COME BACK, ALICE SMYTHEREENE!

It was there, just as Pendleton had said. On page seven of the *Post*, next to an ad for cosmetic surgery.

WHERE, OH WHERE IS THE QUEEN OF ROMANCE?

Acting on an anonymous tip, police were searching today for the million-dollar romance writer, Alice Smythereene. Foul play or just runaway? Your guess is as good as theirs. But it's a fact that Alice doesn't live here anymore. At least not lately.

"She hasn't been around for two weeks," one of the neighbors in her swanky East Side apartment building told the Post. "Saturday night before last I heard some noise from her apartment and what sounded like a scream, so I knocked on her door next morning. She was gone and hasn't been back since."

The scrumptious scribe, known to her friends as Sherry, is famous for her torrid best-sellers, her flaming good looks, and her antics in some of New York's hottest night spots.

"Blockbuster novels from a blockbuster woman," according to a spokesman at her publisher's office.

The cops are keeping mum on this one, but we've learned that they've assigned some heavy hitters to the case. So Sherry, if you're alive and well and reading this, the Post joins millions of your fans in calling out to you: Come back, Alice Smythereene!

COME BACK, ALICE SMYTHEREENE!

N.J. McIver

PaperJacks LTD.

TORONTO   NEW YORK

PaperJacks

COME BACK, ALICE SMYTHEREENE!

PaperJacks LTD.

330 STEELCASE RD. E., MARKHAM, ONT. L3R 2M1
210 FIFTH AVE., NEW YORK, N.Y. 10010

Published by arrangement with St. Martin's Press

St. Martin's Press edition 1985

PaperJacks edition September 1986

This is a work of fiction in its entirety. Any resemblance to actual people, places or events is purely coincidental.

This PaperJacks edition is printed from brand-new plates. No part of this book may be reproduced or transmitted in any form or by any means, electronic or mechanical, including photography, recording or any information storage or retrieval system, without permission in writing from St. Martin's Press.

ISBN 0-7701-0426-6
Copyright © 1985 by N.J. McIver
All rights reserved
Printed in Canada

To Nonie, with love

COME BACK, ALICE SMYTHEREENE!

Chapter 1

Désirée felt her heart pounding as the young Viscomte clasped her in his arms. His kiss took her breath away.
"I adore you," he whispered as their lips parted.

Ugh. Cliché. And "Viscomte" sounds too fruity.

The handsome Baron D'Amante took her hand in his and drew her to him. Désirée shivered as his lips touched hers.

Too flat. Try something a little more sensual.

The Baron's hand cupped her soft, round breast as his lips brushed her neck. The fragrance of mimosa . . .

There was no getting around it; the work was not going well. Alice Smythereene drained the last tepid drops of Budweiser from the can, rose from the typewriter and strode to the television. At a quarter to nine on a Friday night there ought to be a few innings of baseball left to watch.

It was the top of the sixth, and the Mets were losing to Pittsburgh by a score of eleven to three.

Nothing's right today, thought Alice. Nothing's been

right all week. Not since Elaine left. Damn it, how could she have done it?

Alice popped the top of another can of Bud and drank it while making an inspection tour of the apartment's main disaster areas. A coffee stain lay like a large amoeba on the lime green upholstery of the living-room couch. In one arm of the dark brown Queen Anne chair were two cigarette burns, and in front of it a large ashtray lay where it had been spilled two days earlier. On the floor near the doorway were pieces of a smashed vase, a memento of Elaine's departure. And next to the dining table at which Alice had been working, a two-foot mound of crumpled papers—the sludge pile, as Elaine called it— stood like a monument to three days of writer's block.

On the sideboard a large stack of mail waited to be answered. It had been delivered from the Herman Charnoff Agency how many days ago—could it have been last Monday? Alice eyed it with distaste for several moments before drawing a bulky manila envelope from the bottom of the pile. It contained about fifty pages of manuscript held together by a thick rubber band. There was also a letter.

Fort Wayne, Indiana
September 4, 1983

Dear Miss Smythereene, or may I call you Alice,

You have been my favorite authoress for so long that I feel like I know you real good. I fell in love with your books beginning with "The Candlelit Contessa" and I haven't missed one of them.

Now you have inspired me to write one of my very own, a love story, I call it "Princess of the Kankakee" and it is the story of a young woman of royal birth in the time of King Louis (of France) who is kidnapped by a band of Arabian pirates and brought to America where she is raised by a tribe of Indians until a wealthy plantation owner rescues her. Well anyway you can read some of it for yourself because I have sent you the first forty-

seven pages which is all I have wrote what with my job at the motel and two kids to raise.

Gee, I never thought I would have the courage to write and send you this but I can tell from your books that you are a real warmhearted woman. I hope you will be truly honest with me in giving your opinion. All my friends who I have showed it to say my story is good and just like one of yours which thrills me to death because that is just what I was aiming for because you have been my inspiration.

Hoping to hear from you real soon.

*Your intense admirer,
Valerie Hammerscheid*

Alice took the manuscript gingerly between thumb and forefinger, held it at eye level as though inspecting it for maggots, then dropped it on the sludge pile. Inserting a clean sheet of paper into the typewriter, Valerie Hammerscheid's favorite authoress composed a reply.

*New York, New York
September 23, 1983*

Dear Fraulein Hammerscheid,

No, you may not call me Alice. We hardly know each other. In fact you should not even call me Miss Smythereene. The correct form of address in this case would be Mister.

For to be truly honest, Val, I am a man. That's right. A man.

Can you imagine that? The celebrated Alice Smythereene, authoress, goddess of romance and real warmhearted woman, is in reality none other than one Arnold Simon, uncelebrated poet and underpaid professor of literature. Are you surprised? Well, don't tell anybody, because it's a secret.

Right now, O Flower of Fort Wayne, I am hurting bad. My wife has left me, I'm facing a deadline I can't meet and I seem to have lost the ability to concentrate. Not to mention that the Mets are at the bottom of their division and losing yet again. So I find myself reduced to answering banal billets-doux such as yours, and I can't even seem to do that very well.

It is five years now, <u>liebe</u> Hammerscheid, that I have been pounding the typewriter as Alice Smythereene, grinding out the insipid mishmosh of candlelight, mimosa and torn bodices that has had them panting at the paperback racks all over Fort Wayne and the rest of these United States. And why, you ask, have I been doing that? Well—not to put too fine a point on it—for money. To be truly honest, dear Val, I have made a bundle. In fact I have made more in the last two years as Alice Smythereene than I did in the previous ten as a professor at one of our nation's leading universities. How do you like them values, Val?

What do you think, O Daughter of the Middle Border? Does money buy happiness? Here I sit in my Fifth Avenue co-op, owner of a couple of acres in Vermont to boot. Not to mention the old brownstone in Brooklyn Heights I got as a steal eleven years ago. I have every kind of doodad you could imagine—a Mercedes, a Hasselblad, a sailboat, you name it—plus more money in the bank than my immigrant grandparents ever knew existed. All from filling the heads of sweet things such as you full of the most noxious bilge ever to ooze from the diseased soul of man. But am I happy? Well, it wouldn't be too bad if only Elaine would come back.

Anyway, Valerie, that's who I am and why I write the stuff I do. The great mystery is why you or anybody else reads it.

As for your manuscript, I'm quite sure it's awful. But keep plugging, don't let me discourage you.

He stopped typing long enough to pour an inch of Scotch into a tumbler and fill it with water. Already feeling slightly drunk, he sipped the Scotch and reread what he had just typed. Cathartic though it had been, it would not do. Calmer than before, he removed the paper from the typewriter, crumpled it and threw it on the floor. On a clean sheet he began anew.

New York, New York
September 23, 1983

Dear Valerie,
  I hope I may call you Valerie, for I feel that I already know

you. Thank you so much for your very sweet letter. It is knowing how much my stories mean to people like you that is my greatest reward.

As you may imagine, I have been dreadfully busy with my newest novel, and so I have not had time to read your manuscript with the attention it deserves. A quick glance, however, leads me to think you may indeed have potential as a writer, so I am passing your story on to my agent, who will reply directly to you.

Thank you again for writing. It's so nice to know I have such an admirer.

*Your friend,
Alice Smythereene*

Arnold sat back, rubbed his eyes, and decided to call it a day. He felt drained of energy. The hell with the deadline, let Herman worry about it. The hell with Elaine, who needed her? And the hell with Valerie Hammerscheid. He removed the letter from his typewriter, folded it carefully into an airplane and wafted it toward the sludge pile. It missed the mark by several feet, coming to rest on the sideboard next to the set of bone demitasse cups that had been a gift from Elaine's mother.

"Fuck it," he muttered.

It occurred to him that he had not eaten since breakfast. An orgy of Chinese food would be just the thing to revive his spirits. Quickly swallowing what was left of the Scotch and water in his glass, he stood up and weaved toward the door, aiming a vicious kick at the sludge pile as he passed. He missed, lost his balance, and had to grab hold of the sideboard to keep from falling. Remaining for several moments in a bent position, he wavered between resuming his forward motion and sinking to the floor. Then straightening himself, squaring his shoulders and moving slowly but steadily to the door, Alice Smythereene, née Arnold Simon, went out into the September night in search of solace.

Chapter 2

Arnold Simon had been born in Coney Island Hospital on a hot August day in 1943. Alice Smythereene had been born over dinner at Sammy Chu's House of Canton on Mott Street on a cold January evening in 1978. Midwife to her birth had been Herman Charnoff, gourmand, gambler and Arnold's literary agent. Herman had made a killing at the track—or so he claimed—and was treating Arnold and Elaine to one of Sammy Chu's seven-course extravaganzas. Arnold suspected that the real purpose of the dinner was to ease the breaking of bad news concerning his latest manuscript.

"You ought to give it a try, kid," Herman had urged him between mouthfuls of Moo Goo Gai Pan. "Romances aren't so hard to write—a lotta schmaltz, a little sex, pure girl almost gets corrupted by dirty old nobleman then saved by dashing young count. Hell, you can steal the plots from operas."

He paused to lift the cover off a dish of shrimp with lobster sauce.

"Aren't they beautiful? I used to love Chinese food second only to sex. Now they're about even. It shows what age does to you."

"Herman, I can't write that kind of stuff."

"Of course you can. Actually, I think you'd be good at it. I remember a couple of stories I sold for you years ago. One to *Redbook*, I think and where was the other? *True Confessions?*"

"My God, that was fifteen years ago, when I was a student and needed money."

"And now you don't? All I'm saying is, I thought you were pretty good at writing mush. And the stuff today is more or less the same. More sex, more naughty words, maybe you dress it up in costume—old Vienna or the boulevards of gay Paree. But mush is mush. And I think you can write it."

"Herman, how did such a delicate soul as you ever get into such a racy game as literature?" Elaine asked archly, as she watched Herman heft a forkful of shrimp to his mouth.

Herman ignored her.

"Arnie, there's money in it."

He paused to swallow and furrow his brow.

"Which there is not any longer, I'm afraid, in A. A. Carruthers."

So here it is, Arnold thought. The message we've all been waiting for. *Requiescat in pace*, A. A. Carruthers.

"I'm sorry, Arnold, but we have to face facts. There's no more market for the cerebral detective story. Today it's horror they want. You gotta have at least seven mutilated teenagers by the last chapter, or else an incubus that makes blood squirt out of the Cuisinart in some house in Valley Stream."

"What are you telling me, Herman? That nobody's reading detective stories these days?"

"Oh sure, there's still a market for detective stories—not too big, but steady. Only, Arnold, I'm sorry, not the kind you write. Maybe an overaged private eye with a bad case of weltschmerz. You know the type: drinks too much, reads Rilke, beats up young punks. Or else a typical day in the life of a big city police station—some child molesting, a bomb scare, a homo cop to spice things up. You wanna write one of those?"

"I don't know, Herman. It doesn't sound like my kind of thing."

"Then you should try romance, kid. But whatever you do, the fact remains that I can't sell A. A. Carruthers any more. I'm sorry, but there it is. What the hell, Arnie, nine books in twelve years—it's not a bad run. Pack old A. A. away, get yourself a new pseudonym and try a new style."

And later, after they had gone out into the freezing January night, Herman had taken it up once more.

"I still say make love, not gore. There's money in it."

Elaine had been against the idea from the start.

"It's degrading, Arnold," she insisted later that night as they were preparing for bed. "A. A. Carruthers may not have set the world on fire, but he had some dignity and it was fun. Why not just give him a decent burial and be done with it?"

Arnold rinsed his mouth agitatedly and spat forcefully into the sink.

"You mean give up writing novels?"

"What's wrong with just being a poet and teacher?"

"About ten thousand a year less in income, that's what. How the hell are we going to get by? You thought of that?"

"Oh, Arnold, for heaven's sake. A. A. Carruthers only made ten thousand dollars once, and that was eight years ago. It won't make that much difference."

Something about the calm way she brushed her hair as she said it was infuriating. Details about money had always irritated Arnold.

"I'm a writer, not a bookkeeper," he shouted. "And as a writer I have some pride."

He himself was unsure of the meaning of this last

remark, but Elaine seemed disinclined to carry the argument further.

"Aren't you coming to bed?" she asked.

"In a little while. I want to think things out."

Arnold found a bottle of Heineken in the refrigerator and made a tongue-and-swiss-cheese sandwich to go with it. After finishing the sandwich he sat down at the typewriter. When he rose from it at five the next morning he had written a story entitled "How Many Beds Must I Sleep In Before I Find Someone Who Loves Me?" It told of the loneliness of a buyer for a large chain of department stores, and he sold it on first submission to *Tender Romances* magazine.

Within eight months he had written *The Candlelit Contessa,* which sold over two hundred thousand copies in paperback. *Mallory's Mistress,* which followed, had topped half a million. Three years and four books later Alice Smythereene had found herself famous and Arnold Simon had found himself rich.

And now, three years, four books and five months later—Arnold Simon found himself wifeless and depressed as he crawled from pub to pub through Greenwich Village.

Chapter 3

Elaine sat facing him on the settee, laughing and munching an egg roll. Behind her stood Herman, one hand resting on her shoulder, the other at the neckline of her low-cut taffeta gown. Too low cut for Arnold's comfort. The laughter became higher pitched, more silvery, as Herman slid his hand inside her bodice. The blood rushed to Arnold's head. He rose and tried to move toward them, but his feet sank into the floor as if in a sandpit. Sweaty and nauseated, he gave way to despair as he heard Elaine's laughter growing louder, more shrill.

The laughter dissolved into the ringing of the telephone. The dream faded; the nausea remained. Arnold clenched his teeth and battled an impulse to vomit. Then he willed himself to reach for the telephone.

"Hello."

It hurt his head to speak.

"Simon, is that you? My God, it took you long enough to answer."

"Hello?"

"Simon, can you hear me? This is Matthew Pendleton."

Arnold gripped the telephone tightly. His mind moved in and out of focus like the view through a camera lens, but he was unable to stop at the moment of sharpness.

"I'm sorry. Could you say again who you are?"

"Simon, are you crazy or drunk? This is Matthew Pendleton. Mat-thew Pen-dle-ton," he repeated, drawing out each syllable. "Simon, I have to talk to you. It's important."

Arnold wished he wouldn't begin every sentence by saying "Simon." It was monotonous, oppressive.

"Simon, it's about the disappearance of Alice Smythereene. I have some information that might interest you."

"Disappearance? Alice Smythereene?"

"For God's sake, Simon. Don't you read the newspapers? It's in the early edition of the *Post*."

Even over the phone Pendleton's voice carried the odor of stale cigars. Arnold felt the sensation of nausea rise in him.

"Look, can I call you back in a half hour?"

"Simon, I don't think you realize just what the hell this means."

"I'm sorry, but I'm not very well right now. I'll have to call you back."

"Look, it's important for both of us that we get together on this. Believe me, it's not . . ."

Arnold dropped the phone and ran for the bathroom. When he returned ten minutes later the connection had been broken.

In the shower his mind began to clear. It was Saturday. Somehow he felt sure of that and it provided him a rock on which to stand while regarding the marsh of uncertainty surrounding him. He had gone out the evening before in search of Chinese food and had ended up dead drunk in a bar on East Seventh Street learning Yugoslavian folk songs from an old man who reeked of garlic and claimed to be the poet laureate of Croatia. There was not much else he remembered.

He turned the hot water up and let it beat down on the back of his neck. Why was Pendleton calling him? They hardly knew each other. Matthew Pendleton was no more to him than another of Herman's clients, the author of some half dozen lurid sex novels with titles like *Hot Skin,* books like those which old Mr. Brodsky had kept in the back room of his candy store when Arnold was in seventh grade, books to be sneaked into the house and hidden under the mattress. Now they were sold in supermarkets. Elaine detested Pendleton, called him the Sultan of Sleaze and swore that he tried to look down the front of her dress each time they met.

But what did he want? And what did he mean about Alice Smythereene's disappearance? Questions chased one another through Arnold's mind until they made him dizzy. He tried not to think about them until he had had some coffee.

It was there, just as Pendleton had said. On page seven of the *Post,* next to an ad for cosmetic surgery.

> *WHERE, OH WHERE IS THE QUEEN OF ROMANCE?*
> *Acting on an anonymous tip, police were searching today for the million-dollar romance writer, Alice Smythereene. Foul play or just runaway? Your guess is as good as theirs. But it's a fact that Alice doesn't live here anymore. At least not lately.*
> *"She hasn't been around for two weeks," one of the neighbors in her swanky East Side apartment building told the Post. "Saturday night before last I heard some noise from her apartment and what sounded like a scream, so I knocked on her door next morning. She was gone and hasn't been back since."*
> *The scrumptious scribe, known to her friends as Sherry, is famous for her torrid best-sellers, her flaming good looks, and her antics in some of New York's hottest night spots.*
> *"Blockbuster novels from a blockbuster woman," according to a spokesman at her publisher's office.*

Come Back, Alice Smythereene!

The cops are keeping mum on this one, but we've learned that they've assigned some heavy hitters to the case. So Sherry, if you're alive and well and reading this, the Post joins millions of your fans in calling out to you: Come back, Alice Smythereene!

Seated in a booth at the rear of Milt's Eighth Street Grill, Arnold sipped black coffee as he read the story. There was also a picture—a thirty-five-year-old woman leaning forward, an attractive if somewhat hard face surrounded by a mass of blowsy hair and a breathtaking display of cleavage.

"Not much of a loss to literature, is it? You want some more coffee, Professor?"

It was Francine, the waitress, hovering over his left shoulder.

"When I was fourteen I used to dream of having boobs like that. I thought they were the key to wealth and fame."

She sighed as she refilled Arnold's cup.

"Now I know I was right," she added. "Oh, by the way—I don't mean to be a pest or anything, but did you get a chance to look at those poems I gave you a couple of weeks ago?"

Francine studied poetry in evening classes at the New York University School of Continuing Education. A thin, dark girl with wide, brown eyes and hair that hung to her waist, she reminded Arnold of the flower children of a generation past. In her determination to expose her inner life to a world already glutted on sorrow, she wrote poems that were like primal screams. Arnold found them difficult to read.

"I'm sorry, Francine. I've had a bad week. Do you mind if I keep them a little longer?"

"Oh, sure. Long as you want." Then she added pugnaciously, "But you don't have to bother reading them if you don't want to."

Arnold tried to formulate a response that would assure Francine of his interest without offering too much encouragement. His efforts were spared, however, when an elderly man on the other side of the room bawled, "Hey, don't we get no service on this side?" sending Francine hurrying off to take his order and leaving Arnold alone to ponder the meaning of the story in front of him. The picture he knew only too well. He could almost smell the heavy, musky scent of the woman, and it made him shiver. Her name was Sherry Windsor, and she was a self-described model whom Herman had hired two years earlier to be the face and voice of Alice Smythereene.

"The publisher insists on a picture for the cover of *Daughter of Desire*," he had told Arnold. "What am I going to give them?"

"Well, my high school yearbook picture is very flattering and my beard's not too heavy in it, but maybe I look a little young."

Herman had not bothered to smile.

"What about Elaine? Would she be willing to pose?"

"Not on your life. To begin with, she hates Alice Smythereene and everything connected with her. Not to mention that it would undoubtedly blow my cover."

It had been agreed from the start that Alice's identity was knowledge to be shared among only the three of them—Arnold, Herman and Elaine—and each had a stake in protecting the secret. For Arnold, exposure as Alice Smythereene carried the risk of subjecting him to scorn and ridicule within the literary fraternity, while to Elaine the thought of being associated with such an undertaking ranked only slightly above the prospect of contracting a venereal disease. As for Herman, he was convinced that sales would plummet, and indeed the game might well be up, were it known that that "avatar of feminine romanticism," as *Time* magazine had dubbed Alice, was in reality a middle-aged male Mets fan.

On the other hand, there had been no denying the publisher's request. The growing horde of Alice Smythereene fans demanded a palpable symbol of its culture-heroine—a face, a voice, a corporeal reality with which it could identify. So Sherry had been put on the payroll, her picture displayed on several million book covers, her comings and goings chronicled in the gossip columns of the *News* and the *Post*. As Alice Smythereene she had visited bookstores all over America and autographed ten thousand flyleaves. With Herman at her elbow, she had been interviewed on local talk shows from Baton Rouge to Sioux Falls. She was Alice Smythereene in the flesh without ever knowing that Arnold was the spirit. Herman was the medium through which they communicated.

Arnold's thoughts were interrupted by Francine, who had returned, bearing a prune danish.

"I know you like these and I thought maybe you should have something to eat. Besides," she went on as she refilled his coffee cup, "It's almost lunch time. And you don't look so good today. Are you all right?"

Arnold sensed, not for the first time, that Francine had a crush on him. If it had flattered him in the past, today it made him jumpy.

"Well, let's see. My wife has left me. I'm nervous, depressed and can't work. And I have the worst hangover I can remember since I was eighteen. Otherwise I'm just great, Francine. Just great."

"Gee, I didn't know your wife left you. I'm sorry."

She kept her eyes down as she spoke.

"It's not your fault, Francine."

It was time to go, he decided. He slid out of the booth and walked to the cash register.

"Everything okay, Perfesser?" Milt asked as he rang up Arnold's check. Then, without waiting for an answer, he called over Arnold's shoulder.

"Hey, Francine! You better move that car. I seen the meter maid making her rounds a couple minutes ago. Hurry up. Iris can keep an eye on the tables."

Francine and Arnold left the coffee shop together.

"I just bought a new car," she explained. "Well, I mean not a *new* new car. A new *used* car. I thought I could go for drives out in the country sometimes, you know?"

They walked a few steps down Eighth Street before she stopped and turned to him.

"Hey! I have an idea. Tomorrow's Sunday, and the grill is closed. I don't have to work, I mean. Maybe you'd like to ride up to Bear Mountain or something? The weather is still nice, you know? Not too cold. Get your mind off your troubles, you know what I mean?"

Arnold pondered the offer.

"Well, I'd really like to, Francine, but I don't think this weekend's a good idea. There are some things I have to get done. Besides, I don't think I'd be very good company right now. Maybe some other time."

"Oh sure, any time." She was clearly disappointed. "Anyway, if you want to borrow it some time—to get away by yourself, I mean—I'd be glad to lend it to you."

Her eagerness to please embarrassed Arnold, and he was not sorry when they parted company.

The telephone was ringing when he returned to his apartment.

"Simon, I've been trying to reach you for over an hour. You were supposed to call me back. I have to see you this afternoon."

Under Pendleton's aggressive tone Arnold detected a note of anxiety.

"I'm not feeling too well today, Pendleton. Couldn't we get together some time next week?"

Pendleton made a gagging noise.

"Some time next week? Are you kidding? This is important—to you as well as me. You of all people ought to be concerned about what happens to Alice Smythereene. If you get what I mean."

The last remark was too pointed to be overlooked. Arnold wondered exactly what Pendleton knew.

"Well, I guess I could make it this afternoon. Where should we meet?"

"I thought you'd see it that way once you realized it concerned Alice. Believe me, Simon, it's in your own best interests. Yours and Alice's—if you get me."

Arnold wondered if Pendleton was winking broadly on the other end. He envisioned him taking a long draw on his cigar and hoped it was properly carcinogenic.

"You'd better come to my place," said Pendleton, the note of anxiety returning to his voice. "It's safer."

He lived, it turned out, in New Jersey, at least an hour and a half by car from Arnold's apartment. But he was adamant in insisting that Arnold come to him, and it seemed the only way to get him off the phone. They made an appointment for three that afternoon.

After his conversation with Pendleton, Arnold decided to seek the advice of Herman Charnoff. It was Herman's answering service that responded to his call.

"Mr. Charnoff is out of town. We don't know when he'll be back."

Herman had not said anything to Arnold about leaving town.

"When did he leave?"

There was a pause as the operator checked her records.

"We received the message on Thursday."

"Did he say where he was going?"

"No, sir. That's all we have."

Arnold thanked her and hung up. He dialed another number, and, as he waited for a response, he mulled over the coincidence of Herman's being out of town at the very time of Alice Smythereene's disappearance.

"*O-o-o-o-m-m-m-m,*" hummed the receiver. "*Om Vishnu Vishnaya.* Honor to thy inner spirit. The temple of Vishnu the Preserver welcomes your call. The Mahatma Lodha Vishnu Dan is at the moment in meditation and cannot respond in person, but his spirit is with you. At the sound of the tone please state your message and a number where you can be reached. Those in spiritual distress will not wait long for comfort. And remember that this ministry of Vishnu is not without cost. Any donation will bring you closer to the heart of Brahma. *O-o-o-o-m-m-m-m.*"

There was a moment's delay followed by a chime tone. When it subsided Arnold spoke.

"Luther, this is Arnold. I don't have time to horse around. Call me right back, will you?"

He hung up. Ten minutes later the phone rang.

"Luther?"

"Ah, Simonji. Good morning. May the spirit of Vishnu enter and fill you."

"Cut the shit, will you? I don't have time."

The voice on the other end changed to the plantation darkie of old-time movies.

"Wha ah'm sho 'nuff sorry, Massa Arnold. Us niggahs jes ain' got no sense o' time."

"Luther, please. I'm not well."

Luther Washington had undergone several metamorphoses during the eight years Arnold had known him. As a teenage criminal out of the Bedford-Stuyvesant ghetto he had progressed from stealing tape decks out of cars to stealing the cars themselves, and had served one year of a two-to-ten before being paroled into Arnold's custody. It was all part of a project Elaine had gotten him into—teaching creative writing to juvenile criminals—and Luther had been his shining success. Arnold had arranged for his enrollment in New York University and a Ford Foundation grant for his support.

Four years later Luther had acquired a bachelor's degree in literature, a changed speech pattern, a new view of life and no means of support. His first volume of poetry, *Confessions of an Alley Cat,* had been published to some critical acclaim. But poetry, as Luther soon learned, paid more in prestige and satisfaction than in hard currency.

For two years he had been able to keep going on a grant from the National Endowment for the Arts, running a writing workshop for inner-city youth in Brooklyn. And he had given value for money, devoting heart and mind to the task of passing on some of what he had learned and showing his charges a view of life beyond the dirty streets and smelly tenements.

Now the money was no longer there—those who controlled the pursestrings having decided to breed a hardier band of citizens by making them find their own way out of the slums—and what Luther had done for livelihood over the past two years Arnold preferred not to know. The last six months, however, were too striking to be ignored. Luther had rented a store in the East Village and converted the rear into living quarters and the front into the temple of Vishnu the Preserver. From this headquarters he sold a species of foul herb tea and dispensed ersatz Buddhist wisdom to anyone willing to make the most paltry donation to the continuation of his ministry.

Whether he thrived, or even survived, at this game was more than his friends knew. What Arnold did know was that under the name of Lodha Vishnu Dan, which Luther told him with a straight face was the Hindu translation of Luther Washington, he had written a book called *Beloved of Vishnu: Erotic Poetry of the Ganges,* with which he expected to make a killing and which Herman was currently peddling for him.

"Luther," Arnold said into the telephone, "Do you have any idea of Herman Charnoff's whereabouts? Didn't he have an appointment with you this week?"

"Yeah, for lunch yesterday. He stood me up. May the curse of the goddess Kali fall heavily on his descendants."

"Any idea where he's gone?"

"Wherever the horses are running, if you ask me. Man, I wish he'd get moving on my book. I need the bread."

"What about Alice Smythereene? Do you know what's happened to her?"

Arnold had for some months suspected Luther of being romantically involved with the model Sherry Windsor. They had met at one of Herman's parties, and Sherry had made no secret of her admiration for Luther's physique.

"Oh, her." Luther's tone was surprisingly bitter. "Well, I suppose that, having balled every able-bodied man in the city of New York, she's now screwing her way through the provinces."

Arnold winced. The answer did not please him, coming a little too close for comfort. He wondered what Luther actually knew about Sherry's dalliances but decided not to press the matter further.

"How have you been otherwise, Luther?"

Luther was never downcast for long.

"Ah, Simonji, life is hard, but the spirit of Vishnu sustains me. And for a small donation it can sustain you too. All major credit cards cheerfully accepted."

"As long as I don't have to drink any of that horrible tea," Arnold responded. "Look, I have to go. I have an appointment. You'll have to convert me some other time."

"Any time, sahib. You are always welcome. In the meantime—honk if you love Vishnu."

Chapter 4

Arnold could have wished for a less conspicuous car. Not since his adolescence had he driven anything quite so gaudy as this bright orange Volkswagen with its two smashed and rusted fenders. He kept his eyes fixed forward as he drove across the George Washington Bridge, convinced that he was a source of laughter to every driver who passed him.

He had gone to the garage where his Mercedes was kept, only to find it gone. Elaine had beaten him to the punch.

"Your missus was here day before yesterday and took it with her, Cap'n," the attendant told him with an unmistakable smirk. "She said to give you this."

Arnold took the envelope held out to him, but did not open it until he was out on the street. He read as he walked.

Dear Bastard,
You didn't think I'd leave the car for you, did you? Nor is that the only item of mutual property I plan to reclaim, so I strongly suggest you get a lawyer. Which is what I plan to do. And a more competent one than your buddy Hadley Ottinger.
As for transportation, there's always the subway. Maybe your

girl friend has a car you can use. Or is a bed the only equipment she needs?

See you in court.

E.

It was unfair, no question about it, and the reference to his girl friend was especially uncalled for. But what was Arnold to do? The immediate problem was his appointment with Pendleton, and the most reasonable course of action was to call it off, but Arnold could not stand the thought of another telephone conversation with him. Besides, Pendleton's rather pointed allusions to Alice Smythereene had given him cause for concern.

He had walked up Eighth Street pondering his next move until, as he was passing Milt's Grill, a solution had suggested itself.

Francine had been only too happy to lend him her car.

"Don't worry about getting back at any particular time," she had assured him. "I can take the subway home today, and I wasn't planning to use it tomorrow anyway. I can just pick it up on Monday. Besides, I was thinking of going up to Macy's after work to do some shopping, and parking would only be a hassle. Honest, it's fine. Don't worry about it," she concluded over his murmured apology.

Now, as he drove west along Interstate 80, he wondered if he had acted wisely in asking her for the car. The last thing he needed was to get entangled with Francine. Still, there was no getting away from a feeling of indebtedness to her. If the weather continued fine next weekend maybe he'd take a drive in the country with her. It seemed the least he could do.

Pendleton's directions had been clear enough, but Arnold managed nonetheless to lose his way twice after leaving the interstate. By the time he pulled up in front of Pendleton's house he was half an hour late. He got out of the Beetle and looked up and down the street before walking up to the house. For no reason he could explain he felt furtive about his assignation with Pendleton, as though he were expecting something shameful to happen.

The street appeared unusually quiet for a Saturday afternoon. Three houses away a man and a small boy in matching blue jogging suits were tossing a football back and forth across a spacious lawn. Arnold watched the boy throw several passes well wide of the mark and the man cheerfully retrieve the ball each time. Across the street an old geezer in a large straw hat was raking leaves. An ad agency's dream of suburban America—comfortable-looking houses on sizable lots: a placid, lazy neighborhood under the late September sun. Arnold wondered what Pendleton, with his smelly cigars and soft-porn books, had done to merit such a dwelling place.

There was no point in further stalling. Gritting his teeth, he strode up the walk to the front door and rang the bell. His ring was met by silence. After a minute or so he rang again, then banged on the door in case the bell were out of order. He tried to peer through the little glass panes at the top of the door, but the darkness inside was too deep for him to discern anything.

A large black Chrysler, presumably Pendleton's, stood in the driveway, and he walked twice around it, peering at its luxurious interior as if it might offer a clue to its owner's whereabouts. When it did not he decided to try the rear of the house in the hope of finding Pendleton there. He pushed open the gate of the picket fence just in time to see a man leaving the screened porch that ran the width of the house. The man walked quickly toward the rear of the yard.

"Pendleton?" Arnold called to the retreating figure.

The man stopped and turned to face him. Arnold took a few steps forward and then halted. It was not Pendleton.

"Uh, excuse me, I'm looking for Matthew Pendleton."

He was quite the ugliest man Arnold could remember seeing, with the build of a light-heavyweight and a face that looked as though it had hit the canvas once too often—a large, florid face with deep-set squinty eyes and a bulbous nose with a network of veins like a subway map. He stood still for a moment and stared at Arnold, then turned, ran to the back fence, hoisted himself over it and sped away across the adjoining property.

Arnold watched the running figure until it was out of sight. Shaken by the encounter, he wondered if he should look for help. The man looked like a thug, might have been a burglar. On the other hand, he had not been carrying anything out of the house. Arnold decided to ring the back doorbell and then, if there were no answer, seek assistance from one of the neighbors.

The porch door was unlatched. He entered it and walked to a sliding glass doorway, the entrance to the house proper. Through its parted curtains he could see into what appeared to be a den. A black leather couch and two armchairs covered in some sort of white fur were grouped in front of a large television cabinet. The set was on, the sound at full volume. A woman wearing a nurse's cap, her eyes brimming with tears, filled the screen. Through the glass door Arnold could hear her sobbing, "I never meant to hurt you, Dudley."

He rapped several times at the glass door.

"Pendleton, are you there? Hello?!"

He shouted to be heard above the television, but got no response. On impulse he tried the glass door. It slid open at his touch. Abashed at his own boldness he stood in the doorway, his uneasiness growing. On screen the nurse and Dudley were locked in embrace, and Arnold took advantage of the pause in their dialogue to shout into the house, "Pendleton, are you home?" He wondered if there were a Mrs. Pendleton he ought to call out to.

There was something wrong, of that he was sure, and he felt he ought to investigate further in spite of his embarrassment at the thought of intruding. He gingerly stepped over the threshold and walked warily across the den, calling out as he moved.

"Hello, Pendleton? It's me, Arnold Simon."

The den opened onto a large living room—two overstuffed maroon couches flanking a large stone fireplace, windows covered by red brocade drapes that kept the room in semi-darkness. In one corner of the room a man was kneeling in front of a large cream-colored armchair, the upper half of his torso pitched against the seat. Arnold looked in wonder at the man's unusual position until, through the half-light in the room, he noticed dark splotches on the upholstery. There was a smell of smoke.

"Pendleton?"

Without taking his eyes from the figure kneeling at the chair, Arnold groped along the entranceway wall until he found a light switch. As he turned it on his hand trembled slightly. A large floor lamp alongside the armchair illuminated the body at the base of the chair, and now Arnold could see a dark substance oozing from the back of the head just below the hairline.

The doorbell began ringing, a series of loud, deep chimes. Its sound had a galvanizing effect on Arnold. He moved jerkily toward the body until he was close enough to make out its features. The head was turned with its right cheek lying on the seat cushion, the left profile clearly revealed. It was Pendleton, and there seemed little doubt he was dead. An immense gash behind the left ear looked to Arnold, who had never seen a bullet hole, as he would have imagined a bullet hole to look. The skin around the hole looked burned. The hair along the back of the neck was matted with blood.

The ringing had stopped, and now from the rear of the house, where Arnold himself had entered, came a high-pitched, nasal voice riding over the sound of the TV.

"Yoo-hoo, Mr. Pendleton. Are you home? It's Lydia Morgenstern. I'm having a witty-bitty trouble starting my car, and I wonder if you could help me?"

Arnold stood immobile over Pendleton's body, feeling as though he were about to faint.

"Yoo-hoo, Mr. Pendleton. Can a neighbor come in?"

The question was rhetorical, for the speaker had already made her way across the den and was standing at the living-room entrance. Arnold turned to face a gnome about five feet tall with hair the color of rosé wine. They stood silent and motionless for a moment, he and this gnome whom Arnold now recognized as a woman, small and bent, her face covered by a shield of death-white makeup. Of indiscernible age—somewhere between fifty and one hundred from what Arnold could tell—she looked very frail, mouth open and face frozen in a mask of fear.

The silence was broken only by the sound of a commercial for spaghetti sauce issuing from the TV in the den. Arnold took a few steps away from the body as if hoping to disassociate himself from the bloody scene.

"I found him here this way. I had an appointment."

The gnome in the doorway uttered a shrill scream.

"No, please—you don't understand." Arnold tried hard to sound reassuring.

There was no placating her. After a momentary pause for breath she began screaming again, half an octave higher than before. Arnold's impulse was to run. Pushing the gnome to one side he bolted out of the living room and through the den. On his way across the porch he collided with a low, wrought-iron cocktail table, which sent him sprawling on the floor. Picking himself up he hobbled with bruised shin and skinned knee out into the backyard. At the corner of the house he ran into a small gray poodle dragging a leash. He kicked it aside and ran limping to the orange Volkswagen. Just as he reached it, the dog caught up with him and made a lunging attack at his left leg.

"Michelle! Come back here!"

A young girl was calling to the dog as she moved up the street toward them. From inside Pendleton's house the screams came louder. The dog's teeth tore through Arnold's trouser leg and into the flesh of his calf, causing him to cry out in pain. He kicked it away for the second time and managed to get into the car and start the engine. The man in the blue jogging suit ran toward him, and Arnold had to swerve sharply to avoid hitting him. The poodle raced barking after him for half a block.

As he drove away he thought he heard a siren in the distance.

Chapter 5

All the way back to the city Arnold searched the rear-view mirror for signs of police cars but saw none. For a while he thought he was being followed by a large yellow Buick that stayed about three car lengths behind, slowing up when he did, passing when he passed. In his state of nerves he fancied it belonging to the big ugly man with the bulbous nose he had seen in Pendleton's backyard, but the Buick never came close enough to afford him a look at the driver's features. It followed him over the George Washington Bridge then fell out of sight for a time, only to reappear on the East River Drive. Once in an A. A. Carruthers story his hero had shaken off a tail by a clever series of turning and backtracking maneuvers through the city's one-way streets, but here on the East River Drive there was nowhere to go but straight ahead. He left the Drive at 96th Street and drove the rest of the way along the city streets, west to Fifth Avenue and then south all the way home, with several zig-zag east-west excursions en route to throw off the trail. By the time he reached lower Fifth Avenue he felt pretty confident he was not being followed.

His calf and ankle were throbbing when he got home. Roger, the doorman, stared at him in obvious disapproval as he entered the building.

"Are you all right, Mr. Simon?"

Arnold realized for the first time that he presented a somewhat less than tidy appearance. Looking down he saw a large tear in his left trouser leg where the dog had bitten him, and there were bloodstains up and down the right leg of his light gray flannel pants and on the sleeve of his pale blue sweater. Although unaware of touching Pendleton's body, he must, he now realized, have brushed against it more than once.

"I was involved in an accident on the East River Drive," he told the doorman. "That is, I wasn't part of the accident, but I passed right after it happened and I stopped to help. What a bloody mess. Poor devils."

He felt a little ashamed of how glibly he was able to lie.

Upon entering his apartment he made straight for the liquor cabinet and poured himself a tumblerful of Scotch. In the bathroom medicine cabinet he found some codeine tablets left over from a batch his dentist had prescribed six months earlier, and he swallowed one with the Scotch. Next he attended to his wounds. The dog had broken his skin in two places, one on the calf, the other on the heel. He cleaned them with hydrogen peroxide and bandaged them carefully, wondering as he did so about the chance of rabies. Well, there was nothing to do about it. Except worry. He could hardly go back and find the dog and ask to have it tested. Anyway, a suburban poodle like that must have had shots.

In the kitchen he found a note from Elaine.

Dear Arnold,

I came by to pick up a few of my things and to talk to you. I waited an hour but couldn't stay longer.

I have seen a lawyer and she recommends we talk things over before going ahead with legal action. Now that I have cooled down a little and no longer want to emasculate you, I think maybe it's a good idea. At least we can part civilly and not make a hash of everything.

> *I'm still at Beverly's, so why don't you give me a call tomorrrow?*
>
> *Dispassionately,*
E.
>
> P.S. *I took some books and records, but only the ones that were clearly mine. That includes the Toscanini* La Traviata *you gave me on the night you proposed. You bastard.*

He remembered the night he had given it to her—how the two of them had sat holding hands in her parents' living room in Flushing, listening to the voices of Licia Albanese and Jan Peerce. At the end of the record they had held tightly to one another and promised to love forever. The music ran through his mind, mixing with the vision of her, and he felt a tremendous longing. He got up, went quickly to the phone and dialed the number at which she was staying. After twelve unanswered rings he reluctantly replaced the receiver in its cradle. Tomorrow, he told himself, tomorrow he would go and find her and talk to her.

He poured another Scotch and sipped it as he tried to sort out the strange events of the day. Why had he run from Pendleton's house? Why had he felt guilty? It had been stupid—he hadn't done anything. He had been shocked, panicked. But would the police accept that as sufficient explanation for his having bolted?

The police. He ought to get in touch with them right away. After all, he was a witness, had seen that creature with the bulbous nose leaving Pendleton's house. It seemed likely the man was Pendleton's murderer. Arnold shuddered as he recalled how close they had stood facing one another. Thank God the man's instinct had been to run. What if he had decided to attack him, kill him on the spot?

Yes, it was important that he notify the police. But he had better get his story straight first. They would want to know why he had been at Pendleton's house. What should he tell them about Alice Smythereene? About Sherry Windsor? It might get sticky.

He tried to think of the whole thing as an A. A. Carruthers novel and pictured himself talking to the police, saying something like "Inspector, to begin with, I am the real Alice Smythereene!" It lacked the ring of plausibility.

The codeine and Scotch had made him drowsy. It was hard to think. He stretched out on the wide, comfortable couch to mull things over. If only he could discuss it with Elaine. So sensible, so levelheaded. She would know what to do.

Elaine. His thoughts returned to the night he proposed to her. If only she were beside him now, holding his hand. The music of *La Traviata* welled up in his mind, the voice of Jan Peerce. He sang softly, under his breath.

Di quell'amor, quell'amor ch'è palpito
Dell'universo, dell'universo intero.

The words were kitsch, all about love, the pulsebeat of the universe. Well, he could use a little kitsch right now. He ached for Elaine.

Tomorrow, he thought. Tomorrow I'll go see her. It was his last thought before falling asleep.

Elaine's friend Beverly Michelson lived in Brooklyn Heights on the third floor of a brownstone owned by the Simons. The first two stories housed a clinic and counseling center for disturbed children run by Beverly and Elaine. In former years, before Arnold had struck it rich, the Simons had occupied the second floor. Then, almost simultaneously, the clinic had expanded and Arnold had been overcome by an itch to move to swankier surroundings. The move had been opposed by Elaine.

"We can move the clinic," she had told him. "There's a suite of offices on Montague Street that Beverly looked at, and she says it would suit us fine. We can move the clinic there and rent out the first floor of the brownstone as an apartment. Or better yet, we can move down to the first floor and rent out the second. It'll help cover payments."

But Arnold was firm. For some time he had had his eye on a cooperative on lower Fifth Avenue, and now that Alice Smythereene was a success he wanted to make the move. It was convenient, he had argued. He could walk to work.

"Well, I can walk to work here," Elaine had countered. "Besides, we've lived here for more than ten years. Most of our friends live around here. I like this neighborhood."

In the end Arnold had won out. It was over a year since they had made the move, but somehow Elaine had never accepted the change. Looking back Arnold wondered if he hadn't made a mistake, if moving from Brooklyn had not perhaps been the first touch of frost on their relationship.

He decided to take the subway over to Brooklyn. On a Sunday morning it was not likely to be crowded, and the muggers and perverts would, he hoped, be enjoying their day of rest. Besides, he had found a reasonable parking space for Francine's car, one that was good until mid-morning on Monday, and he was reluctant to tempt fortune by moving it.

He rode to Court Street, then walked the few blocks to Beverly's apartment. On entering the subway he had purchased a bunch of large yellow chrysanthemums, which he had held in his lap during the ride and which he now carried tucked in his right arm. In his left hand he carried a sack of croissants. The day was beautiful, one of those sultry, sunny mornings that can make the end of September such a poignant time. Across the street from him a young mother was pushing a baby carriage past a closed pornographic movie house. A group of swarthy teenagers were clustered around a pizza stand, eating large pieces of pizza as they argued raucously but good-naturedly in Spanish, while on the curb in front of them a grizzled old man sat drinking from a bottle wrapped in a brown paper bag.

Come Back, Alice Smythereene! 33

As he turned down Schermerhorn Street and walked the last two blocks to his destination, Arnold began to feel slightly nervous. He had not called ahead and felt less confident of his reception than when he had set out from home. Then it had seemed only natural that Elaine would be as glad he had come as he would be to see her. Now that the encounter was imminent, he was not so sure. It occurred to him that she might not even be home.

A plate on the door read "Brooklyn Heights Center for Adolescent Development," and next to it were two door buzzers. Arnold pressed the one marked "B. Michelson" and waited. After a minute he rang again. From a third-floor window a voice shouted "Just a minute. I'll be right down." It was Elaine. Arnold took a deep breath and tightened his grip on the bag of croissants.

She opened the door wearing a quilted pink housecoat with large white flowers. Although it was almost noon, she had an early morning new-waked look that Arnold had always found irresistible. He wanted to drop the croissants and chrysanthemums and take her in his arms. Instead he held the bouquet out to her and said, "I brought you these. And some croissants."

"Oh," was all she answered. Then, after a few moments, "Thanks."

"I hope I didn't wake you."

"No. I mean yes. I mean, it doesn't matter. I couldn't sleep very well last night, so I got up and watched TV until it got light. Well, anyway, it doesn't matter."

"I couldn't sleep last night either."

It was a lie. Arnold had slept like a log on the couch. But it seemed like a good thing to say. Besides, he probably would not have been able to sleep had it not been for the state of exhaustion he had found himself in after his adventure at Pendleton's house. Not to mention the Scotch and codeine.

They looked at each other in silence for the space of a minute or two until Arnold asked, "Can I come in? I mean for coffee or something? I brought some croissants."

He held the bag toward her. She laughed.

"Yes, I know. You already told me."

The house had a backyard of sorts, a courtyard really, about the size of a squash court. Its most memorable feature was a crab apple tree they had looked on from their bedroom window when they had lived there, which exploded into a breathtaking burst of pink blossoms for a week or two each spring. Now, of course, there were no blossoms, and the ground was littered with the decay of dozens of miniature apples. They had always taken Sunday breakfast there in fine weather, and it was to the yard that they now repaired for coffee and croissants. The old Adirondack chairs were still there, in need of painting and uncomfortable as ever. They aroused in Arnold a sense of nostalgia for some happier time now gone. He perched on the edge of one of them and looked earnestly at Elaine.

"I was really hoping for a chance to talk to you like this. I want to ask . . ."

"Elaine, are you out back?"

It was Beverly's voice coming from inside the house. The back door opened and she stepped into the garden.

"I'm back with the *Times*. I thought you'd still be asleep, so I—Oh, my goodness. Hello, Arnold."

"Hello, Bev."

She advanced a few steps into the yard carrying the Sunday *Times*. Then she stopped and looked at them in embarrassment.

"What's the matter with me? You two must want to be alone. I'll just take a few sections of the *Times* and go upstairs."

Good old Bev, thought Arnold.

"Don't be silly, Beverly," said Elaine. "Come and sit down. Arnold brought us croissants."

"Oh, I think I ought to—"

"Beverly, sit down," insisted Elaine.

Casting an apologetic glance at Arnold, Beverly settled into a vacant chair. Declining Elaine's offer of a croissant, she slipped the *Book Review* out of the *Times,* dropped the rest of the paper on the ground beside her and read assiduously as Arnold and Elaine made halting conversation.

"How's your work going?" he asked.

"Oh well, you know, about the same. We hired a new counselor who's not working out, but I guess we'll manage. How's your new book?"

"Not coming along very well. I haven't been able to concentrate. And now with the disappearance, and Herman out of town, I'm not even sure if I should continue."

"Disappearance?"

"Uh. Alice Smythereene's. Um—you know. Sherry Windsor."

He could hardly bring himself to say the name. It came out in almost a whisper. Elaine's eyes widened and her face set in a look of anger. From behind the newspaper Beverly snorted.

"Oh God, I'm sorry," Arnold stammered. "I didn't mean to . . ."

He left the sentence unfinished.

"Forget it," said Elaine. "Water under the bridge. Well, you might as well tell us about her disappearance as long as you've opened that particular can of worms. A permanent disappearance? Or is that too much to hope for?"

He did not know why he had assumed they would have heard of it. Neither Elaine nor Beverly read the *Post* or watched the news on television very often, and the story would hardly have appeared in *The New Republic* or *The New York Review of Books* or any of the other sources from which they learned of the world's doings. He told them the story of the phone call from Pendleton and of his grisly visit to Pendleton's house. If he had wanted their attention he could not have found a more effective means of capturing it. Beverly dropped the paper onto the ground, and they both stared at him in shocked surprise.

"My God," Beverly said when he had finished. "Have you told the police?"

"No, not yet. Everything happened so quickly. I needed some time to think. Get my story together, decide exactly what I ought to tell them."

Elaine made an impatient gesture.

"What is there to decide? Just tell them what you saw."

"Well, it's more complicated than that. They're going to want to know why I ran away. Also what I was doing there, and that's going to lead to questions about Alice Smythereene's disappearance and about my, er, connection with Sherry Windsor."

Elaine stiffened at his words. They sat in uncomfortable silence, not looking at each other, until Beverly spoke.

"What about your leg? Have you seen a doctor?"

Glad for the change of subject, Arnold showed her the wound and the homemade dressing he had applied to it. Beverly, who had been a nurse, insisted on taking him inside the apartment to re-dress it.

"I think you ought to talk to a doctor about rabies shots," she told him. "My guess is you won't need them, but it might be good to find out."

When they returned to the backyard Elaine spoke to him in a calm, determined voice.

"I realize there are certain things that may come up in an investigation to cause you some embarrassment. But it seems to me you have no choice but to tell them what you saw."

Her eyes narrowed.

"Besides, facts are facts. There's no wishing them away. And if they make you squirm . . ."

Her voice faltered.

"Couldn't you just tell them you dropped by to visit Pendleton?" asked Beverly.

"I don't see how. We didn't know each other very well. I was never at his house before, didn't even know where he lived. It'll seem too fishy."

Elaine agreed. "I don't see the point in lying. You have nothing to hide. You haven't done anything illegal."

Arnold noticed the way she emphasized the last word but let it pass unremarked.

"Look," he said, "I intend to report to the police. All I want is a little time to sort things out in my mind. After all, my behavior at Pendleton's house, just my being there for that matter, may seem suspicious to them. So I have to be prepared to answer a lot of questions, and I'm not sure how much background I want to tell them. Personal things, I mean. And it's not as though there's an undiscovered murder. I'm sure they've been all over the place, taking fingerprints and whatever else they do. A day's delay won't make much difference to them. Besides, I'm not even sure whom to report it to. It happened in New Jersey. Do I report it to the state police or the locals? Or should I go to the New York police and let them notify New Jersey? Maybe I should call Hadley Ottinger first and get some legal advice."

Elaine threw up her hands.

"Yes, that's what I'll do," he went on. "First thing tomorrow morning I'll call Hadley and get his advice. Maybe ask him to accompany me."

"I hate to mention it, Arnold," said Beverly, "but has it occurred to you that this man might be dangerous? To you, I mean. If you're the only one who saw him . . ."

"Of course it occurred to me." He shivered slightly, recalling the ugly face with its mean, deep-set eyes. "But I don't see how he could possibly know who I am. Look, I promise you I'll go to the police not later than tomorrow morning. Now can we drop the subject?"

He turned to Elaine with a pleading look.

"There are other things I'd like to talk about. Could we go for a walk?"

They strolled, he and Elaine, along the Promenade. The wind had risen and there was a slight chill in the air. The bay was choppy but the air was clear, and the Lower Manhattan skyline stood resplendent on the other side. He took Elaine's arm as they walked and she did not draw away.

"Elaine, I'd like you to come back and give me another chance. I know I was wrong, but it was the first and last time, and I just can't get along without you."

The last words were almost drowned by the whooping laughter of two girls on roller-skates gliding past them.

"I don't know, Arnold. You hurt me very much. When I came into that hotel room and found you in bed with that—that slut . . . I . . ."

They had paused at the railing and stood facing across the bay to the Battery. Elaine turned her head away from him. Arnold was silent, not knowing what to say.

"Then after we were back in New York," she continued, "And we had had it out and you told me how she meant nothing to you, how it had all been some mid-life anxiety fling—after you told me how much you loved me—after all that to find the two of you in our apartment, you passed out on the couch, her half-undressed on the floor next to you. In our own apartment, Arnold. Really!"

"Elaine, I told you that wasn't my fault. The first time in Chicago, yes. I wish I could take it all back, start again, but I can't. But the next time, in the apartment, that was nothing. I mean, nothing happened. I mean there was no intention for anything to happen. Oh hell, Elaine. You had gone to Connecticut to visit your sister, remember? I was home working. She called and said she wanted to see me, said she had a way to help me make things up between us, between you and me. She wanted to come up to the apartment, but I said no. So we agreed to meet for dinner. It was dumb of me, I know, but I was kind of desperate for any kind of help I could get, and I didn't see what harm could come out of meeting for dinner. Besides, after what had happened it didn't seem, well, polite to turn her down."

"Polite? You went out with her to be *polite*? You have one hell of a sense of chivalry, Arnold."

"It was only going to be one time, just for dinner. We had a few drinks, I remember that. Then something happened to me. I must have gotten sick or something. Honest, Elaine—it was as though I'd been drugged. I couldn't walk, could hardly sit up. She had to take me home, and I guess I passed out. That's all I remember until you walked in and started a row."

"Gee, I'm sorry to have made a row," Elaine rejoined icily. "I guess I forgot my manners. Imagine that. And you such a stickler for politeness."

"Aw, come on, Elaine. Give me a break."

They walked back in silence. When they reached the end of the Promenade Arnold stopped, put both of his hands on her arms and turned her toward him.

"Elaine, I love you. I never loved anyone in my life but you. I don't think I can live without you. Please come home with me."

There were tears in her eyes. She moved against him and buried her face in his shoulder. After a few moments she straightened up.

"Could I borrow your handkerchief, please?"

She took it from him and wiped her eyes. Then she looked at him.

"I love you too, Arnie, but I'm not ready to come home yet. Maybe in a few days. I have to think things over some more."

It did not escape him that she had called him Arnie. It was a hopeful sign, the best he was going to get that day. It would have to do.

They were about fifty yards from the house when Arnold saw the man on the stoop talking to Beverly. He stopped in his tracks and stared as the man turned, descended the steps and walked down the street away from them.

"Oh, my God," whispered Arnold.

"What's the matter?"

But Arnold did not stop to answer. He took off, walking quickly in pursuit of the man, who by this time had turned the corner and was out of sight.

Elaine walked the remaining distance to the house by herself. Beverly was still standing in the doorway, and she and Elaine waited on the stoop until Arnold returned a few minutes later.

"I lost sight of him, God damn it. He must have ducked into some building or down a subway entrance."

He turned to Beverly and asked gruffly, "What did he want here?"

"Why, he was just asking for directions. Wanted to know how to get to the Academy of Music. Why? What on earth is the matter?"

Both women looked at him questioningly. Elaine frowned.

"Arnold, what the hell is wrong with you? You look as though you've seen a ghost."

"It was him. The guy with the bulbous nose. The one from Pendleton's garden."

Chapter 6

On Mondays Arnold taught his first class at eleven o'clock, and he customarily indulged himself by sleeping until ten. This morning, however, he woke at seven-thirty. There were things to do. First he must call his lawyer. With luck he could reach him at home before he had left for the day. He hoped Hadley would have time to accompany him to the police. At least he would know the best way to proceed.

The appearance of the man with the bulbous nose and deep-set eyes had added a sense of urgency to the business of notifying the authorities. At the same time it strengthened Arnold's determination to seek advice before proceeding further. How had Pendleton's murderer, if that was indeed what he was, known to look for him in Brooklyn? At the very house he owned? Not from staring at him for a few seconds in Pendleton's backyard, that was for sure. The inference had to be made that Arnold was involved in Pendleton's death in some deeper way than he understood. And in some way, he felt certain, connected with the disappearance of Sherry Windsor.

He sat in his pajamas on the edge of the bed and looked at the telephone. How much, he wondered, ought he to tell Hadley? As with Beverly Michelson the previous day he wanted to be as frank as possible, but some circumspection was required. Neither knew, for example, of his activities as Alice Smythereene. Well, perhaps it was too late to keep that secret. Things had taken too grim a turn. He decided to call Hadley and play it by ear.

As he reached for the telephone the house phone rang. He walked barefoot into the foyer to answer it. It was Roger, the doorman, announcing a visitor.

"A young lady, Mr. Simon. Says she's come to get her car keys."

Roger's tone betrayed his skepticism.

"Okay, Roger, send her up."

The doorbell rang as he was rummaging through his closet for something appropriate in which to receive Francine. Giving up, he slipped a bathrobe over his pajamas and walked barefoot to the door.

"Oh gosh, you were asleep. It didn't occur to me." Francine was flustered. "It's just that I pass this building on my way to work, and I knew you lived here. So I thought I'd save you a trip to the grill. In case you weren't planning to come in anyway, you know."

"It's okay, Francine. Come in a minute while I find your keys."

It occurred to him that he must have left them in his bloody trousers of two days before. He had stuffed his clothes into a corner of the closet, not sure of what to do with them.

"I think they're in the bedroom," he told Francine. "Wait here a minute."

As he groped along the floor of the closet he heard her steady stream of chatter from the living room.

"Wow! What a beautiful apartment. The view is fantastic! I can see Washington Square Park. I've never been so high up in an apartment before. Wow!"

He found the keys and replaced the pants in the back of the closet. When he returned to the living room he found her gazing in awe at a large lithograph.

"Gee! Is that a real Dufy?"

"Well, it's only a lithograph. They're not all that expensive, you know. We found it in a shop near the Luxembourg Gardens, and . . ."

"In Paris? You mean Paris? Wow! It must be wonderful going to Paris and buying works of art and all."

It had been their first trip to Europe. Arnold remembered how Elaine's command of French obscenities had charmed the proprietor to the point where he had served them coffee and reduced the price of the lithograph to one that Arnold could hardly resist. Still he had refused, pretending to think it too expensive for them—which indeed it was in those days—and the next day when she went off to visit the Orangerie he pleaded a headache, and, as soon as she was gone, made straight for the shop and bought the Dufy. It had been waiting on her pillow when she returned to the hotel.

The remembrance gave him a twinge of sadness that must have shown in his face, for Francine, who had turned her gaze from the lithograph to him, said, "I guess it must be tough with your wife gone and all."

Her words snapped him back to the present.

"Oh, I'll be okay, Francine. Listen, thanks a lot for the car. It was a . . ."

He was about to say it had been a lifesaver when it struck him that the phrase was not altogether felicitous in light of his experience.

"Look, uh, Professor Simon."

She paused as if waiting for him to say, "Call me Arnold."

"Call me Arnold," he obliged.

"Arnold."

She savored the name like a mouthful of the purest Colombian coffee. It made Arnold feel uncomfortable.

"Arnold."

"That's me," he said, as jauntily as he could. "Me Arnold. You Francine."

His attempt at humor was lost on the girl, who stared

at him soulfully, her lip trembling. He felt like a cad. He wished he had not borrowed her car.

"It must be awful with your wife gone, Arnold. Lonely. I know what that's like. If there's anything I can do to help, anything at all, I want you to know that I would consider it—well, a wonderful privilege."

She had advanced several steps closer and was almost touching him.

"Look, Francine, it's not that I don't appreciate . . ."

He started to back away, but she restrained him by placing her hand on his arm.

"Arnold, seeing you every day, hearing your voice . . . If you were my man I would never leave you."

She had moved her arms around him. She was so close he could feel the pumping of her heart as she reached up and kissed his lips. Behind him he heard the sound of a key turning in a lock and the front door being opened.

"Jesus Christ!" Elaine swore softly, almost in a whisper.

Arnold jumped back, out of Francine's embrace.

"You son of a bitch!" Elaine had found her full voice. "You dirty, lying bastard. Well, don't let me interrupt anything."

She turned and strode from the apartment, slamming the door as she went.

"Elaine, wait!"

Arnold ran out of the apartment after her. He caught up with her at the elevator.

"Elaine, it's not what you think. Believe me. It was nothing. Nothing happened."

She was crying.

"That's what you said the last time, you bastard. Now that your sweetie has vanished you've gone right out and gotten someone else. You're not even a decent cheater, you know that, you creep?"

"Elaine, please.'

The elevator had arrived. He kept his palm against the rubber moulding of the door to keep it from closing.

"Elaine, you've got to listen to me."

"I listened to you yesterday, didn't I? 'I love you, Elaine, I can't get along without you, I'm sorry, it'll never happen again.' Then I stayed awake half the night worrying about you, frightened about that thug who's after you. So this morning I canceled all my appointments just to get here early and make sure you were all right. I thought maybe I would go to the police with you so you wouldn't have to face it alone. But you obviously weren't expecting me."

"God damn it, Elaine, it isn't what you think!"

"Let go of that elevator door, Arnold, or I'm going to start screaming and make one hell of a scene."

It dawned on him that he was standing in the hallway barefoot and in his bathrobe. Feeling foolish and unnerved, he dropped his arm and allowed the elevator door to close.

"She's young enough to be your daughter, you pervert," was Elaine's last shot at him as the door slid shut.

"That's not true." Arnold was stung by her last remark. Then, as an afterthought, he shouted at the closed door of the elevator, "I'll call you tonight and explain everything."

Francine stayed for breakfast. No more harm could come of it, it seemed to Arnold, than had already happened. And he needed someone to talk to, the chance to explain himself. So he put off calling his attorney, and instead made coffee and toast and scrambled eggs while she cleaned up the week's accumulation of dishes. Not that that had been necessary. Arnold assured her that Mrs. Boggs, his cleaning lady, would be in on Wednesday, but Francine insisted. It gave her something to do, a means to cover her embarrassment. About Elaine she was contrite to the point of self-flagellation.

"Now I've gone and ruined your life," she told Arnold, keeping her eyes on a blackened pot she was trying to scrub clean. "Killed your chance for a reconciliation. You must hate me."

She seemed on the verge of tears. Arnold, who was not much of a cook, had no time to comfort her, devoting all his attention to keeping the eggs from overcooking as he scraped the burnt toast.

"Maybe I could go and explain it to her. How it was all my fault, how you don't even know I exist most of the time, you know? Maybe I could make her see that it really wasn't your fault."

The thought of sacrificing her own happiness for the domestic tranquillity of the man she loved seemed to buoy Francine a bit. Arnold shook his head.

"It wouldn't do any good. You see, the trouble is she, uh, found me before. With another woman, I mean." It was Arnold's turn to avert his eyes. "That's why she left me in the first place."

He scraped the overcooked and shrivelled portion of eggs out of the pan and onto two small plates on the butcher-block table. Then he took two of the newly washed mugs from the draining rack where Francine had left them a few minutes earlier, placed them, still wet, on the table and filled them both with coffee. He motioned an invitation to Francine to sit down and eat.

"I'm not much of a hand at scrambled eggs," he murmured apologetically.

Francine was silent. She still looked surprised at Arnold's admission of infidelity. He felt the need to elaborate.

"It was Sherry Windsor. The woman who disappeared a few days ago. Uh, she's the author of the Alice Smythereene books."

He was not sure exactly how much he wanted to reveal. But what he had already said produced a marked reaction from Francine. She stared at him open-mouthed for a moment before saying in an awed voice, "You mean you *knew* her?"

Arnold smiled.

"Both in the biblical and non-biblical senses, Francine."

"Wow!" was her only response. Arnold could not tell if her reaction was one of shock at the thought of a sensitive intellectual like him consorting with a commercial hack, or if she were bowled over by his having had carnal knowledge of such a celebrity.

"Well, I didn't know her all that well," he went on. He wanted to talk about it. There was relief in putting it into words, even to so unlikely a confessor as Francine.

"We had met a few times at parties and flirted a little. She was a terrible flirt. Uh, *is* a terrible flirt, I guess. Well, I suppose I flirted too. I've been having some trouble coming to grips with my age—turning forty, I mean—and I guess it flattered me to think I could attract the attention of a, um, sexy woman."

It had also amused him, although he did not confide it to Francine, to flirt with the public embodiment of his own mythic creation. The knowledge that she was not Alice Smythereene and that he knew it and knew, in fact, who was and she did not, gave him a sense of power, a sense of being in on a secret, which now, in retrospect, seemed shabby.

"But nothing happened between us. I guess I really didn't want anything to happen. A little flirting at parties to make me feel sexy and younger, you know. but nothing that would actually lead to anything. Until we met by accident in Chicago a month or so ago."

He paused to drink up the coffee in his cup, then he poured another for each of them. Francine did not take her eyes off him.

"It was my birthday," he went on, "and I was scheduled to read a paper at the summer meeting of the M. L. A. The Modern Language Association. It's the trade organization of English professors. I was going to talk on 'Symbols of Aging and Death in the Poems of W. E. Henley.' Can you imagine? On my fortieth birthday, when I was feeling the cold breath of aging and death on my own skin. Not a very cheering prospect. I wanted Elaine to come with me, to hold my hand through the whole ghastly experience. God, it sounds stupid, doesn't it? But that's the way I felt. It really bothered me, turning forty. And the thought of facing it alone in a strange city was getting me down.

"Anyway, Elaine wouldn't come. She couldn't get away from her work, or so she said. I got sulky, and we parted not on the best of terms. So there I was in Chicago, an 'aged man . . . a tattered coat upon a stick,' as Yeats put it, presenting my paper to a roomful of sharks just waiting to sink their teeth into my little treatise and rip it to shreds, then off to dinner on my own to try and console myself as best I could. When who should turn up but Alice Smythereene herself. Sherry Windsor, I mean. Staying at the same hotel, no less. She was in Chicago to do some book promotion. I asked her out to dinner, we ordered a bottle of champagne to celebrate my birthday. We flirted a little. Then I got really bold and asked her up to my room."

As he spoke he remembered the scene in the hotel restaurant, the heady smell of her perfume, the sense of her nearness, his desire to touch her. They had bantered, flirted, joked—joked about virility after forty, about marital infidelity as a cure for middle-aged boredom—and he had had the sensation of standing at the edge of a high cliff and staring at the dizzying depth beneath him. A feeling like vertigo, which had both scared and excited him. When she had accepted without hesitation his half-serious suggestion that they spend the night together, his first sensation had been one of fear. Like a game that had suddenly turned too real but from which there was no dignified way of backing down.

In his hotel room she had been surprisingly tender. He had experienced what is referred to in the pop psychology magazines as a case of performance anxiety. It was, after all, the first time in some fifteen years of marriage to Elaine that he had embraced another woman. Sherry had been patient and had coaxed him to a successful completion of the adventure, but in truth he had to admit he had not cut an impressive figure.

"The thing I didn't know," he continued to an attentive Francine, "was that Elaine was planning to surprise me in Chicago that very night. So when she walked into my hotel room hardly a few minutes after Sherry and I had, uh . . ." He waved his hands helplessly. "Well, I was really surprised."

There was a moment's silence as they looked at one another. Then Francine asked, "Is that what she walked out on you for?" Her tone of incredulity made Arnold aware of the difference in their ages and of the fact that somewhere in that fifteen-year span had occurred a sexual revolution that stood between their two generations like a continental divide.

"Well, actually there was another incident," he admitted. "After we got back to New York things were pretty tense between us. I tried to explain to Elaine how I had felt, but not with much success. Maybe I didn't understand it myself. I guess we're both more conventional than we liked to believe, and I was a little shocked myself at what I had done. I don't know if that makes any sense to you."

Francine continued to stare at him. He saw himself reflected in her eyes in the act of changing, of aging like the portrait of Dorian Gray. Except that instead of appearing more evil and dissolute he imagined himself becoming more stodgy and dull as he unfolded his tale of middle-aged marital woe.

"It wasn't clear if Elaine was going to stay with me or not. I was trying desperately to convince her not to leave me, but she claimed she needed to get away and think things over. So she went to spend a week with her sister in Connecticut. She hadn't been gone two days when Sherry called and wanted to see me. She talked very reasonably on the phone, said she was sorry if she had caused trouble between me and Elaine, and said she had an idea how to put things right. Of course I was skeptical, but I wasn't doing too well on my own and had half-convinced myself that Elaine was being unreasonable. At any rate, the long and the short of it is that I agreed to meet Sherry for dinner.

"I was pretty nervous about seeing her, and fortified myself with a couple of Scotches before starting out. So I was already a little high by the time I met up with her. I kept drinking during dinner and really got tanked. I just about passed out in the restaurant. It was as though I'd been drugged—I had no control over my own body, couldn't walk, couldn't even sit erect. God, I must have made a spectacle of myself. I remember Sherry and the headwaiter getting me into a taxi. Then I must have passed out, because the next thing I remember is waking up on the couch, Sherry on the floor alongside me and Elaine standing at the entrance to the living room making a horrible row. She was crying and shouting, and she smashed a vase on the floor."

He remembered that the pieces were still lying where Elaine had thrown it. They had bought the vase on Cape Cod the summer after they were married, and it was the artifact they had owned longest as a couple. Arnold winced to think what its shattering symbolized with regard to their marriage. He resolved to gather up the pieces and try to reassemble them into their original state before Mrs. Boggs came in and swept them up with the trash.

Francine was looking at her watch.

"Oh, my God!" she exclaimed. "It's nine-thirty. I was due at the grill an hour ago. Milt'll kill me. I gotta go.

Thanks for the coffee, Professor. I'm sorry about your problems with your wife."

He had made the transition, Arnold noted, back to Professor. Like Wordsworth, he had outlived his romantic appeal.

He showed her to the door, remembering at the last minute to tell her the whereabouts of the car.

"It's parked on Tenth Street just west of Fifth," he called out to her as she waited in the hall for the elevator. "It's good until noon, but the street becomes a no-parking zone after that. I'm afraid you'll have to put it in a garage for the rest of the day."

After the elevator door had closed behind her it occurred to him that he should have offered to pay the garage fee, for she undoubtedly would not have incurred it had she not lent him the car. He thought of trying to catch up with her downstairs to make the offer, but decided on reflection that it could wait until he saw her at the grill at lunchtime. He had had, he thought, enough of women for a while.

Chapter 7

There was over an hour left before he was due in class, and Arnold took advantage of the time to take a long, hot shower, then shave and dress. As he did so he pondered what to do next. Should he go to the police? And if he did, how would he explain his behavior at Pendleton's house two days before? And how much should he reveal about Alice Smythereene?

He called Herman but was once again connected to the answering service, who had no more news than they had given him on Saturday. He was on the point of phoning Hadley Ottinger when the doorbell rang.

A black man about six feet six, gray-haired and broad-shouldered, stood filling the doorway. He held out a badge for Arnold's inspection.

"Detective Sergeant Henry Farner, sir. New York Police Department. I told your doorman not to bother announcing me. May I come in for a few minutes?"

Arnold's heart sank. How had they found him so soon?

"No. I mean yes, come on in. Oh, but I have a class in half an hour."

He waved his hand vaguely toward the living room and allowed the detective to precede him into it. His legs felt weak, his stomach queasy. It had been a bad mistake, he realized, not to have contacted the police earlier. Now it would look as if he had something to hide. He had an impulse to blurt everything out, tell all he knew at once. Or perhaps it was wiser to tough things out, say nothing unless asked. He wished he could speak to Hadley and wondered if he would be allowed a phone call.

"This won't take but a few minutes," Detective Farner assured him. "But before we get down to business I'd like to tell you what a privilege it is to meet you, Professor Simon. I very much enjoyed your article on Thomas Hardy in the *New York Review of Books* a few months back, and I thought your point about Hardy's repressed sexuality was very interesting."

Arnold stared at him in amazement.

The policeman chuckled. "Myself, I always wanted to be a writer. Graduated from City College with a major in English and got one year toward a Master's degree at Columbia under my belt before I ran out of money. Ah well, I've got no complaints. Not when I think of what's happened to some of the fellows I grew up with. At least I've got a steady job and my work's useful, or so I like to think. And I do get to see plenty of things worth writing about."

Arnold searched his mind for an appropriate response but came up empty. After a short pause and a sigh the detective continued.

"Well, sir, to business. I'm investigating the disappearance of Alice Smythereene, the writer. I understand that you are a friend of hers, Professor."

"I wouldn't say that," Arnold answered quickly. Too quickly, he decided. "I knew her slightly, met her at a few parties. We had the same literary agent."

Farner seemed not to be listening. He had moved to the bookcase while Arnold was speaking and was now eyeing the poetry volumes.

"Well, my, my. Edward Arlington Robinson. A much neglected poet, don't you think?"

He began to quote, apparently from memory.

> So on we worked and waited for the light,
> And went without the meat and cursed the bread;
> And Richard Cory, one fine summer night,
> Went home and put a bullet through his head.

Then he turned to Arnold and, hardly missing a beat, went on to say, "Your doorman says she brought you home drunk on the night of Friday, the sixteenth of September. That's a week ago last Friday."

Arnold felt as though he had been hit in the stomach. He silently cursed Roger for a traitor and regretted he had not taken Elaine's advice and been more generous in his tip the previous Christmas.

"Did you say last Friday? Oh no—the Friday before last, wasn't it? Let me think."

He was stalling for time and felt foolish. Better to admit the truth, he decided. After all, he had nothing to hide.

"Well, yes, come to think of it. I did see her that night. We went out for dinner. I had too much to drink and, er, passed out in the taxi. She brought me home."

"According to the doorman, your wife found the two of you here and made quite a scene."

On second thought he should not have given Roger any tip at all. The ungrateful swine.

"I don't see how he could know anything about that since he was seventeen stories below in the lobby."

"You've got a point there, Professor. I guess his claim is that she stormed out of the building almost as soon as she came in."

"My wife is a highly emotional person."

It was all Arnold could think of to respond. It seemed not to matter, however, for the detective's attention had returned to the bookcase. He was thumbing through a volume of Poe from which he began to read in a deep bass voice

> "Wretch," I cried, "thy God hath lent thee—by these
> angels he hath sent thee
> Respite—respite and nepenthe from thy memories
> of Lenore;
> Quaff, oh quaff this kind nepenthe and forget this
> lost Lenore!"
> Quoth the Raven, "Nevermore."

The interview was taking on a surreal note, Arnold thought. The detective replaced the book and turned back to him.

"Well, sir, it would be nice if we could just forget this lost Lenore. Or, rather, this lost Alice—or, to be more precise, this lost Miss Sherry Windsor. But this particular raven has the job of saying nevermore."

"Look, Lieutenant . . ."

"Sergeant."

"Whatever. I've only got fifteen minutes to make my class. And I really don't think I have any information of use to you."

"You're right, Professor. I've kept you too long. Let me just leave you my card in case you think of anything that might be helpful."

Arnold took the card and slipped it into his wallet without looking at it. He began gathering up his material for class, but was stopped by the detective's next question.

"Have you been in Chicago recently, Professor?"

Arnold felt a moment of panic. Then, collecting himself, he struck out on a course of righteous indignation.

"Look here, Sergeant, am I under suspicion for something? If so I would like you to tell me so that I can call my lawyer."

"Oh my goodness, no. Nothing like that, sir. It's just that Miss Smythereene—I mean Miss Windsor—was in Chicago a few weeks ago, and I happen to know, since I follow these things, that the Modern Language Association was meeting there at the same time. I thought perhaps you might have run into her there."

Arnold was not sure how much Farner knew and whether he was playing some game with him, but he decided to bluff it out.

"I was there, in fact. I gave a paper on Henley. But I certainly did not see Miss Smythereene. Nor Miss Windsor."

The detective's chuckle was heartier than the joke merited. Arnold felt unnerved by the interview. He wondered whether Farner was going to ask him about Pendleton. Surely the detective must be aware of the murder. Perhaps it was out of his jurisdiction. Arnold wished he had written police procedurals so that he might be more familiar with the workings of the system.

Farner cast a last wistful look at the bookshelves before heading toward the door.

"I certainly envy you your collection of books, Professor Simon."

Then, looking around the large, expensively furnished living room, he added, "And your apartment. Perhaps I should have stuck it out to a Ph.D. Being an English professor seems a much more lucrative occupation than I would have thought."

"I have other sources of income," Arnold replied testily.

"I'm sure you must," said the detective.

In the doorway he turned back and looked once more at Arnold.

"Oh, by the way, Professor, you don't own an orange Volkswagen, do you?"

Arnold froze, but managed to keep his composure.

"No, I do not."

"Well, good-bye then. Please don't forget you have my card in case you think of anything that might be helpful."

As he closed the door Arnold realized he had handled the interview badly. Why had he felt so guilty when, in fact, he had done nothing wrong? Well, as Elaine had put it, nothing illegal, at any rate. It had been stupid of him to put off notifying the police about his visit to Pendleton's house, but he could hardly believe that a two-day delay constituted a criminal act. As for Sherry's disappearance, he knew no more about it than anyone else who had read Saturday's *Post*. Except that Pendleton had been involved and had sounded nervous, even a little frightened, on the phone. But what did it have to do with him?

Arnold's class did not go well that morning. To begin with, he was late. The interview with the detective had left him little more than five minutes to collect his material, wait for the elevator to carry him to street level, then sprint down Fifth Avenue and across Washington Square Park, a sequence of actions that under optimal conditions required a quarter hour. He arrived at the classroom ten minutes late, in the nick of time to prevent his audience from dispersing into the inviting September sunshine. The bolder ones were already pawing the ground in the hallway, while the more timid sat on the edges of their chairs, ready to join the stampede as soon as it began. Arnold managed to corral them, but the mood had soured. They were restless, sullen at having missed the chance to escape.

He had, in his haste, forgotten his notes and was forced to extemporize. The course was devoted to a survey of poetry, the students a mixed lot of would-be accountants, pharmacists, statisticians and such, all undergoing their mandatory brush with culture before assuming their places in the mercantile world. Arnold fell back on the traditional trick of unprepared English teachers: reading aloud. He possessed a robust baritone voice that lent itself well to the bardic verses of Dylan Thomas.

> Dressed to die, the sensual strut begun
> With my red veins full of money,

he intoned, images filling his mind as he did. Pendleton's red veins had been full of blood that had turned all sticky and matted at the base of his neck. Had he been dressed to die? Arnold's own red veins were full of money, the lifeblood of Alice Smythereene feeding the cells, fueling the twentieth-century middle-class myth of romance. And what of the sensual strut? The smell of Sherry Windsor's scent came unbidden to his nostrils, and he saw her naked on the bed of his hotel room in Chicago, her breasts heavy and liquid as she lay back and waited for him to mount her.

His mouth was dry. He swallowed, then read on.

> In the final direction of the elementary town
> I advance for as long as forever is.

The elementary town meant, of course, the cemetery. On another level, death itself. Again he thought of Pendleton. Perhaps he was at that very moment being buried. Where? And by whom? He was the only dead person Arnold had ever seen in a natural state, without benefit of the mortician's cosmetic touch, and it bothered him somehow that he knew so little about the man.

The room must have been overheated, for he was sweating by the time he had finished reading. He looked up from his book and out across the rows of students, trying to judge the effect of the poem on them. In the first row were his two best, Miss Carlucci and Mr. Slatkin, he a soft, blubbery boy, sensitive, insecure and very responsive to literature, she a rock of common sense, salty and combative. He turned his glance toward them as he closed the book. Miss Carlucci was engrossed in a crossword puzzle. Mr. Slatkin was asleep.

Milt's Eighth Street Grill was crowded by the time Arnold arrived. It was the height of the lunch hour, and Milt, at his usual perch behind the cash register, was showing signs of strain.

"Francine ain't here, Perfesser," he called out to Arnold immediately on seeing him enter. "She picks one hell of a time to decide she gotta move her car. Over a half hour she's been gone."

The place was full, there was a small line of people waiting to be seated, and Iris, Milt's wife, was having trouble coping by herself.

"She was also an hour late this morning," Milt went on, airing his complaint to the clientele at large. "I mean, everybody's entitled to their fun and relaxation. I ain't sitting in judgment on nobody." This last sentence seemed to be directed at Arnold in particular. "But I got a business to run."

Milt's litany was cut off by a piercing whine. Through the plate-glass window of the restaurant Arnold saw a police car race down Eighth Street followed closely by an ambulance. The screaming of their sirens filled the cafe for a brief instant, making conversation impossible, then died away down the street. Milt's attention, which had been diverted from Arnold by the noise, was now claimed by several patrons wishing to pay their checks.

Arnold decided not to wait for a table. He wasn't all that hungry, his chief purpose in coming having been to reimburse Francine's garage fee, and he supposed that could wait until a less crowded hour. As he turned to leave, the door was thrown open from the outside, and Arnold was almost knocked down by an enormously fat man who pushed past him into the room, calling out to no one in particular, "Hey! Did you hear the racket a couple of minutes ago? Some broad just practically blew herself up in her car. It smashed a window over on Tenth Street. Shattered it. I'm surprised you didn't hear nothing."

Arnold remembered uneasily that he had parked Francine's car on Tenth. He left the restaurant and walked quickly up Eighth Street to Fifth Avenue, then turned north and ran the two blocks to Tenth Street. To his right as he reached the corner he could see a crowd assembled halfway down the block. Two police cars and a fire engine were parked in the middle of the street, and a barricade had been erected at the corner to prevent cars from entering. As he moved toward the scene Arnold caught snatches of conversation from the fringes of the crowd.

"Just went up boom, like that."

"Well, I heard this noise, like a bomb or something, and the next thing I knew there was glass all over the place, and then Mrs. Livorni, that's my boss, she started yelling to everybody to keep calm, and then . . ."

"It's the fucking Porto Ricans again. I say let them have their God-damned independence."

As he reached the site of the disturbance, Arnold saw two policemen keeping the crowd back from a roped-off area in the middle of the block. On the other side of the cordon a third policeman was talking to a slim Oriental youth.

"That's the kid who saved her," said a voice at Arnold's side. The speaker was a buxom lady of about fifty wearing a gray sweatsuit, her hair in curlers. "I saw it all from my apartment window. She got into the car, poor thing, and then there was a big noise and a lot of smoke . . ."

"And flames. Don't forget the flames," chimed in a wizened man in a Yankees training jacket.

"There were no flames, not right away. Just smoke," insisted the lady in the sweatsuit. "Then this kid came running up and pulled open the car door and dragged her out. Can you imagine that? And him so slight built and all."

"I seen flames," insisted the little old Yankee.

"After. After, there were flames. First there was just smoke."

Arnold pushed his way past them and through the crowd to the rope. One of the police cars started to move away, east down Tenth Street, giving him an unobstructed view. There in the middle of the block, cordoned off from traffic and flanked by a fire engine and the remaining police car, stood the burned remains of the battered orange Volkswagen.

The sight of it stopped his breath. He stood and stared, unaware of anything around him until the gruff voice of a policeman snapped his concentration.

"Hey, buddy, do you mind stepping back? We're trying to keep the area clear."

"How did it happen?"

"Come on, step back, huh? You can read about it in the paper."

"Could you tell me what happened to the girl in the car? I think I know her."

The policeman gave him an exasperated look before turning to a group of firemen standing in back of the hook and ladder.

"Hey, can one of you guys talk to this man? He says he knows the victim."

One of them approached and after a short conversation told Arnold the name of the hospital to which the car's occupant had been taken. In exchange he took down Arnold's name, address and place of employment. Arnold thanked him, then turned and walked back up the street through the dissolving knot of people.

He was not surprised by what he had seen. From the moment he heard the announcement at Milt's Grill he had felt a sense of disaster, a flash of instinct warning him what to expect. Still, the sight of it was something else. As he paused at the corner of Fifth Avenue to wipe his brow he saw that his hands were trembling.

Chapter 8

He waited at the hospital over two hours for news of Francine, shuttling back and forth between reception desk and nurse's station before coming to rest in a waiting room alongside the emergency entrance. An Hispanic family shared the room with him, the woman large and heavily perfumed, sitting with her face in her hands, crying quietly. Her small, wiry husband tried to comfort her, speaking to her softly in Spanish. Next to him stood three immaculately groomed young children looking confused and frightened. Arnold felt uncomfortable, as though the room were their home and he an uninvited visitor come to spy on their sorrow.

After a while he began to feel terribly hungry. He had not eaten since his breakfast with Francine, and then he had only had a piece of burnt toast and a few forkfuls of cold scrambled eggs. It seemed days ago, that breakfast. Indeed, so many strange things had been compressed into the past few days that thinking of last Friday was like looking through the wrong end of a telescope, and he had difficulty putting the events in perspective. It seemed reasonable to assume that the attempt to blow up Francine's car, if that was indeed what had occurred, had been directed at him. He thought of the man in Pendleton's garden who had turned up so surprisingly on the steps of the house in Brooklyn Heights. That the second appearance was a coincidence was too absurd a notion to entertain.

Arnold was also at a loss to relate Pendleton's death to the disappearance of Sherry Windsor. How were they connected, or, for that matter, were they connected at all? There had been no mistaking Pendleton's inferences on the telephone on Saturday. What had he actually known, and how was that related to his murder? The thread of events was difficult to follow. There was no apparent skein of cause-and-effect.

There was a doctor in the room now, his chair drawn up in front of the Hispanic family, talking to them in low tones. The woman had begun to sob audibly, and the man kept nervously stroking the head of the smallest child. Arnold left his seat and moved as unobtrusively as he could to the exit. A large nurse moved past him in the hallway, as grim and full of purpose as a battleship.

"Excuse me," Arnold called out to her, but she sailed heedlessly by. He walked quickly until he came alongside, then fired another "Excuse me" like a warning shot across her bow. She stopped and turned to face him.

"Excuse me," he repeated. "Is there any news of the young lady who was brought in here a couple of hours ago after her car exploded?"

The nurse looked at him as though he had just demanded that she perform an unnatural sex act.

"Name?" She threw the question at him like a challenge.

"Arnold Simon," he replied, wishing he were not so easily intimidated. The nurse bore an uncanny resemblance to Mr. Amalfitano, his high school wrestling coach, who had made Arnold's life hell for two years before they had both concluded that he was intended by nature for gentler pursuits.

The nurse had reached the admitting desk and was thumbing through the cards of that day's arrivals.

"We have no one here by the name of Arnold Simon," she said with an air of closing the case. Was she mocking him, Arnold wondered.

"That's not her name, that's my name. Hers is Francine."

"Last name?"

He could not remember her last name.

"Are you a relative?"

"No, just a friend."

"I can't give out any information except to members of the immediate family. Now if you'll excuse me."

On reflection Arnold decided that the comparison had been unfair to his wrestling coach.

"You're blocking the desk, sir," was the nurse's last salvo at him. "You'll have to wait in the waiting room."

It seemed like a good time to go for lunch.

Outside he bought a newspaper and looked around for a place to eat. Alice Smythereene had made the front page. Under a headline screaming MISSING AND MURDERED—WERE THEY LOVERS? was a picture of Pendleton and Sherry seated side by side at what looked like a nightclub table. Judging by Sherry's appearance he guessed the picture was several years old.

Arnold found a kosher delicatessen and feasted on a pastrami sandwich, french fries and a club soda. As he ate he read the story in the *Post*. It contained several surprises. To begin with, Pendleton and Sherry Windsor had known each other better than Arnold had been aware. The newspaper tried to make as much of their acquaintance as possible and to link Sherry's disappearance with Pendleton's murder. With few facts at its disposal it hinted nevertheless at an affair between the two. FATES LINKED BY PASSION? was one of the subheads. What was established, once one had separated fact from conjecture, was that the pair had been seen together a number of times at New York night spots and had spent a few weekends at the house of friends in the Poconos.

More surprising was the information that Pendleton had had a prison record. Under his real name, which turned out to be Mario Parente, he had been twice arrested and once convicted ten years earlier for dealing in narcotics. The newspaper tried hard to play this angle also, but in the apparent absence of any real evidence had to fall back on the statement that "Police would not comment on allegations that Pendleton's death is linked to drug traffic." Whose allegations, Arnold wondered. Most likely the rewrite man's at the *Post*. There seemed no end to what one could hint at in this vein, and Arnold amused himself while waiting for a piece of apple strudel by inventing a few of his own, such as "Police failed to respond to rumors that Pendleton had been a transvestite K.G.B. agent" and "Authorities neither confirmed nor denied suggestions that Pendleton was tickled to death by invaders from the planet Krypton."

The strudel turned out to be delicious, and Arnold decided to indulge himself in another piece while he perused the sports pages. The baseball season was winding to a close. Soon it would be time to put the boy who lived inside him into hibernation for the winter. For some reason he thought of Auden's lines.

> Now the leaves are falling fast,
> Nurse's flowers will not last;
> Nurses to the graves are gone,
> And the prams go rolling on.

Damn, he swore silently, interrupting his own train of thought. Must every poem I think of these days be connected with death?

He turned for relief to the entertainment section of the paper. Perhaps he could find a movie to go to that evening. Something funny, something that would keep his mind from wandering back to death and police and hospitals. As he scanned the page his attention was caught by a small item in a column of TV gossip. "ABC said today that despite the author's disappearance it was going ahead with production plans for a mini-series based on Alice Smythereene's block-buster novel 'Mallory's Mistress.'" That was news indeed! Arnold had never heard of a mini-series based on *Mallory's Mistress*. Herman had never mentioned it. Surely he must have known.

It occurred to Arnold that Sherry Windsor's disappearance must be linked in some manner to this latest discovery. Some publicity caper concocted by Herman to maximize the coverage given to the start of production. It was the sort of thing Herman would do, with or without the consent of the network. Once, years before, when he had been handling the ghost-written memoirs of an antiquated movie he-man, Herman had arranged for a paternity suit to be filed against the actor. It had filled the newspapers and kept the book high on the best-seller lists for weeks, after which the suit had been quietly dropped. The actor, who had been over seventy at the time, had been delighted by the increases in sales and in his reputation for virility.

A publicity stunt would explain Sherry's disappearance and also the absence of Herman who, having set the plot in motion, was lying low to avoid embarrassing questions. But what of Pendleton? Why had he been killed? Could it, after all, have been coincidence? Some connection, as the *Post* implied, with the drug trade, something arising out of his unsavory past? That still did not explain his calling Arnold on the telephone to talk about Alice Smythereene and his hints of inside knowledge about Arnold's relation to that authoress.

Of course, if he had been Sherry's lover, or even her friend, Pendleton would have known that she was not the real Alice Smythereene. But how would he have known anything further? It was at this point that Arnold had to come to grips with a thought that had been gnawing at the fringe of his consciousness for the past several days. The idea had been growing in his mind that perhaps he had told Sherry more than he intended about his double life as Alice Smythereene—had, in fact, given the show away. He was fairly certain he had revealed nothing in Chicago. At least nothing explicit, although now that he thought of it, it did seem that his attitude had been a shade too cute. He had been unable to resist a few innuendos that a clever person might have picked up on. As for his date with Sherry in New York, there were too many blank spaces in his memory for him to feel any confidence in his discretion on that evening.

There was no point in thinking about it. What was done was done, and he would have to wait for Sherry's reappearance to find out what she knew about him. In the meantime he had other things to worry about.

By the time he got back to the hospital the Hispanic family was gone from the waiting room. In its place were two teenage girls, chewing gum and talking in very loud voices. Arnold went off in search of news and was able to find an intern willing to discuss Francine's case.

"Superficial burns, some cuts from flying glass and a bad case of shock. We've given her a sedative and we'll keep her overnight for observation. But all in all, she's okay. Good thing the Volkswagen's engine was in the rear. If she had been in a front-engine car she probably wouldn't have any legs right now."

Two orderlies came wheeling a stretcher down the hall. On it lay an elderly man whose face was a deep shade of blue and whose breath came in loud, agonized gasps. The doctor fell in line behind and followed them to the treatment area. Left to himself, Arnold debated the wisdom of trying to see Francine. The admitting clerk was busy taking particulars from a middle-aged woman who had brought in the old man on the stretcher. Back at the waiting room the two girls had been joined by a boy in a leather jacket carrying a portable radio. Arnold decided not to wait.

That evening he telephoned Elaine but was unable to talk to her.

"She's asleep, Arnold," Beverly told him. He was not sure whether to believe her or if it were a ruse of Elaine's to keep from talking to him. In either case there was not much he could do about it.

Beverly was not unsympathetic as he recounted the events of the day: the visit from the detective, the bomb in Francine's car.

"I must say, Arnold," she commented wryly when he had finished, "the women who tangle with you certainly come to grief in one way or another. One disappears, another gets blown up in her car. You're something of an *homme fatal*, Arn."

Arnold was not amused.

"I don't know what you mean by 'tangle' with me. Francine came up to get her car keys, for crying out loud. At seven-thirty in the morning. There I was at dawn, unwashed, unshaved, practically unconscious. I could hardly have tangled with an English muffin at that hour. It wasn't my fault she decided to get amorous."

"You must have something, Arnold."

"What I've got right now is trouble, Beverly. Enough for two people."

He sighed.

"Look, would you just tell Elaine she got it all wrong this morning, that I love her, that . . . Ah, hell. Just tell her I called, okay?"

"Sure, Arn. I'll do what I can." Her voice softened. "Look, hang in there. Things'll work out."

Arnold wished he could believe her.

Chapter 9

Tuesday was Arnold's busiest morning. A series of appointments with students to discuss their progress on term papers followed by a department meeting. At ten he found a few minutes to call the hospital for news of Francine and was informed that she had been discharged. No information on her condition could be given over the phone, but he took her release as evidence that her injuries were not serious.

It was hard to concentrate on his work, but he tried to keep his attention on the job at hand rather than on the dire happenings of the last few days. It was important, he felt, to stick to routine and not lose touch with reality. After his afternoon class he would stop at Milt's Grill and get Francine's address. Maybe visit her that evening. At least send flowers.

Detective Sergeant Henry Farner was waiting just inside the doorway when Arnold arrived at the classroom.

"I hope you don't mind, Professor Simon, but there were a few questions I wanted to ask you, and as long as I'm here—well, I'd certainly enjoy the opportunity to sit in on your lecture before we get down to business."

The man is unbelievable, Arnold thought. But he managed to smile and point to an empty seat at the rear of the classroom.

"No, no, of course not. You're welcome to sit in if you want. Although I daresay you'll find it rather dull stuff."

"I'm sure I won't, indeed, sir." The detective smiled back at him, and, in an exaggerated conspiratorial whisper, added, "Just as long as you don't inform the authorities that I'm cheating the taxpayers out of an hour's worth of my salary to indulge my taste for literary discussion."

Arnold wished the man would behave in a more professional manner and drop the pose of *littérateur*. He turned from Farner and walked to the front of the classroom. The subject of the course was late-Victorian poetry, and once again Fate had chosen to hector Arnold by serving up another poem of love and death. This time of prison as well.

> He did not wear his scarlet coat,
> For blood and wine are red,
> And blood and wine were on his hands
> When they found him with the dead.

Arnold read the stanza aloud, then launched gamely into a discussion of Wilde's poem. From time to time he caught a look at Farner sitting forward attentively, ready, it appeared, to join the discussion at the first sign of encouragement, but Arnold looked away each time, unwilling to let the big detective participate.

> Some kill their love when they are young,
> And some when they are old;
> Some strangle with the hands of Lust,
> Some with the hands of Gold.

At a few places in the poem Farner mouthed the words as Arnold read aloud, as if he knew parts of it by heart. Afterward, when the classroom had emptied of all but the two of them, he waxed enthusiastic.

Come Back, Alice Smythereene!

"Thrilling, Professor Simon. A truly thrilling class. I wouldn't have missed it for the world. You read beautifully. And *The Ballad of Reading Gaol* is one of my very favorite poems. The policeman in me, I guess. What was it that happened to the fellow in the poem?"

"Fellow? You mean the narrator? That's Wilde himself."

"No, no. The one with the blood and wine on his hands."

"Oh. He was hanged."

"Of course. How forgetful of me." And he recited from memory:

> But who would stand in hempen band
> Upon a scaffold high,
> And through a murderer's collar take
> His last look at the sky?

He kept his eyes fixed on Arnold as he intoned the last two lines. Then he added, "Of course, we don't hang people nowadays for murder."

It was time to protest, Arnold decided. He would not allow himself to be the victim of a cat-and-mouse game. Before he could say anything, however, Farner resumed speaking in a businesslike tone.

"And now, sir, if you're not too busy, I wonder if you could indulge us by accompanying me to police headquarters. A few of my colleagues would like to join me in asking you some questions. It shouldn't take too long."

The words "police headquarters" rang ominously in Arnold's ears. He imagined himself on an uncomfortable stool, a bright light shining in his face, rough voices barking sharp questions at him. He had written a number of such scenes as A. A. Carruthers, and, although he had no idea if such interrogations ever actually took place, they were vivid enough in his imagination to frighten him.

"Look here, Sergeant Farner. I don't mind cooperating with you, even though I don't see what information I could possibly have that would be of any use to you. But if we're going to police headquarters, I think that I would like my lawyer to be present."

He was a little surprised by his own assertiveness but decided to press his rights. Farner was unfazed.

"Of course, Professor Simon. You can telephone him from headquarters, first thing as soon as we get there."

"I think, if you don't mind, that I'd like to call him before we leave so that he can meet us there. My office is just next door and I can phone him from there."

Farner seemed hurt by Arnold's lack of trust but made no objection. He waited in Arnold's office during the call, walking back and forth in front of the bookshelves and making admiring comments under his breath. Hadley Ottinger was not in, but he was expected back soon. Arnold explained the situation to Ottinger's secretary, and it was arranged that the lawyer would leave for police headquarters immediately upon returning to his office.

"Can you tell me exactly where you'll be?" the secretary wanted to know.

"Where I'll be? Oh. Hold on a minute. Where will we be?"

The last was directed at Farner who appeared to be lost in a volume of Gerard Manley Hopkins. The detective must have heard him, however, for without looking up from the book he replied, "Just tell him to come to One Police Plaza and ask the clerk for Henry Farner, special unit number three."

As he repeated the information over the telephone Arnold wondered what a special unit signified.

The interview was not at all what Arnold had expected. No light in his eyes, no cigar smoke, no sound of rubber hose smacking against the palm of a burly copper pacing back and forth. Instead he sat in an imitation leather armchair in a carpeted office at police headquarters facing a thin, sixtyish man behind a large walnut desk. Farner and another, younger man sat on a couch.

"I'm Captain McPartland, NYPD special unit number three, Mr. Simon. We appreciate your coming down here and giving us a little of your time."

It was on Arnold's tongue to question whether he had had a choice in the matter, but McPartland continued without pause.

"I ought to tell you that we have already talked to Miss Francine Havlick, and we know you borrowed her car on Saturday—a car that matches the description of one seen at the house of Mario Parente, alias Matthew Pendleton. I think it would be wise of you to tell us just what you did on that day and also what you saw."

A uniformed police officer brought in a carafe of coffee and several cups and saucers and placed them on a low table in front of the couch. Farner poured a cup and carried it over to Arnold.

"I hope you take it black, Professor. We don't seem to have any cream."

"Oh, that's fine. Thank you."

There was a moment of silence as Arnold sipped the coffee. It was very hot and strong. The man behind the desk broke the silence by asking, "Well, Mr. Simon, what can you tell us about Saturday?"

It was better to tell the truth, Arnold decided. At least most of it. He told them of the phone call from Pendleton—omitting any reference to Alice Smythereene—and of his visit to Pendleton's house. He described the big ugly man he had seen in the backyard, recounted his discovery of the body and his encounters with the gnome lady and the poodle, and told of his impression of being followed on the way home. McPartland and Farner kept their eyes on him the entire time he spoke. The younger man on the couch took notes in a steno notebook. Arnold could not tell if they believed his story.

"Why didn't you use your own car?" Farner asked when he had finished.

"My wife took it away. We're, er, separated. She took the car."

"Are you and Miss Havlick very good friends?"

That's none of your business, Arnold wanted to say. Instead he answered, "No, not very. I know her from the coffee shop."

"Then the appointment must have been very important to you if you borrowed the car of a relative stranger in order to keep it."

Arnold shrugged. "I had nothing else to do."

McPartland gave him a piercing look.

"Come, come, Mr. Simon. You'll have to do better than that. What did Parente want to see you about? What was so urgent that you borrowed a car and drove out to New Jersey?"

Arnold took a moment to collect his thoughts. The time had come, he supposed, to tell the whole story—his double life as Alice Smythereene, his little affair with Sherry. He felt rather foolish, but, after all, what he had done was no crime.

His silence must have been interpreted as a refusal to answer, for McPartland shot a new question at him.

"What do you know about Big Augie Mancuso?"

Arnold had never heard of him.

"Vinnie Viola? Does that name mean anything to you?"

"Does he play baseball?" asked Arnold. "I remember a utility infielder for the Cincinnati Reds about ten years ago . . ."

McPartland cut him off.

"Mr. Simon, I think things will go better for you and for all of us if you'll just be straightforward. Now surely you can tell us something about Augie Mancuso, can't you?"

Arnold shook his head. Farner took up the questioning.

"Professor, you live in a very expensive apartment.

Expensively furnished, too. I hope you won't think I'm prying if I ask how you manage that on a professor's salary?"

"I write," Arnold answered defensively. "Books."

"Ah, yes." McPartland read from a paper on his desk. "Writer of mystery novels under the pseudonym A. A. Carruthers. Last novel published in 1977."

"Very well written books, if I may say so," Farner interjected. "Implausible stories, of course. But a real way with words."

He was silenced by a look from McPartland, who resumed the questioning.

"Surely you're not asking us to believe that a minor writer of detective thrillers makes enough money to maintain a fancy apartment on lower Fifth Avenue. Not to mention a summer house in Vermont. And a Mercedes."

Arnold resented being called a minor writer. He also objected to the tone the interrogation was taking. It was time to assert his rights.

"I refuse to go on with this until I've seen my attorney. I am a citizen of the United States and a lifelong resident of New York City. I pay my taxes on time. I . . ."

The telephone on McPartland's desk was ringing. The thin detective answered it and listened to the party on the other end for half a minute. Then he hung up the phone and spoke to Arnold.

"Your attorney's here, Mr. Simon. You're free to go."

Hadley Ottinger and Arnold Simon had known each other since the days twenty years earlier when they had both been Yale undergraduates. Their relationship had been a steady one, if not especially warm or deep. Arnold found the lawyer too overbearing and self-satisfied for his liking, and their friendship had needed periods of lessened intimacy now and then to restore it. At this moment, however, Arnold could not have been gladder to see anyone.

"Dear God, I thought you'd never get here," he told Hadley as they walked out of the building together.

"Sorry, Arnie, but I was in court all afternoon. Then Charlie Brubaker insisted on our having a drink together. Pompous old son of a bitch, but one can hardly refuse him. He'll probably be the next District Attorney."

It was past four o'clock, and the day had become cool. Hadley buttoned his black topcoat against the chill. The coat had one of those velvety collars Arnold found too fruity, but it gave Hadley a definite air of success. Arnold himself was coatless and felt cold. He turned up the collar of his tweed sports jacket.

"I could use a drink myself, Had."

"I'll bet you could. Let's find someplace decent."

They had reached Ottinger's car. As he turned the key in the lock, the lawyer said to Arnold, "I have a better idea. Let's drive up to my place. I'm through for the day downtown. We can take off our shoes, have a couple of stiff drinks, then I'll whip us up something to eat. And you can tell me what this is all about."

Arnold knew that Hadley loved to cook and prided himself on his skill at it. He had once made the half-serious claim that his first marriage had fallen apart because of his wife's jealousy of his culinary ability.

"She was such a flop in bed that when she realized she couldn't even be numero uno in the kitchen her behavior became impossible," he had told Arnold. And then added, "Poor baby. I hope she's found something she can do."

As they headed north in Hadley's Porsche, Arnold turned to his friend and asked. "Hadley, who the hell are Big Augie Mancuso and Vinnie Viola?"

"Damned if I know," his friend replied. "Why?"

Arnold told of his interview with the police. He also related the events of the past few days, from Pendleton's initial phone call to the bombing of Francine's car, once again withholding the vital information about his relationships with Alice and Sherry. That would have to come, of course, but he preferred to wait until they were comfortably settled in Hadley's house.

Hadley lived outside the city in Larchmont, in a large house that stood on an acre of ground. It had been purchased during the tenure of Hadley's first wife, Sonny, a woman of extravagant taste, who had decorated it in a style referred to by Elaine as late bordello.

"She was not the sort of woman a Yalie ought to have married," Hadley had said after the break-up, and he had hired a decorator to redo most of the interior in an exquisitely tasteful if somewhat impersonal manner. One of the rooms that had escaped the decorator's leveling eye was a small downstairs bathroom Sonny had covered in textured wallpaper of satiny black and metallic gold. It featured a full-length mirror in a gilt frame. Arnold washed his hands at the sink, with its two golden swans for faucets, then examined his appearance critically in the mirror. He thought about Hadley and Sonny and about himself and Elaine, and he wondered if he would go the way of Hadley. After the divorce from Sonny, Hadley had taken up with a nineteen-year-old Barnard student he had represented in an accident suit. She had moved into the house in Larchmont and stayed for about a year before running off to Denver with the bass guitarist of a second-rate rock band. Hadley had then married the ex-wife of one of his colleagues. Arnold and Elaine had hardly gotten to know her. The marriage had lasted a little under a year.

Hadley had a Scotch on the rocks waiting for him when he came out of the bathroom.

"Why don't you take this into the den and sit down and relax while I cook dinner. I thought I'd make something simple, maybe a couple of steaks."

With Hadley nothing was simple when it came to food. Arnold anticipated a lengthy wait.

"Oh, and by the way, there's a manuscript on the desk I'd like your opinion on. If you're in the mood for reading, that is. And help yourself to more Scotch when you're ready. You know where it is."

Hadley was also a spare-time writer of mystery novels. This common interest had been the basis for their friendship in college, and Arnold, who had achieved publication first, had brought Hadley into the professional ranks by introducing him to Herman Charnoff some twelve years before. Hadley had a series of books about a character named Rick Rheingold, a smart and tough New York lawyer whose wits were sharper and whose nerves were icier than any of New York's finest, and who, at least once every fifty pages, went to bed with a gorgeous actress or svelte society dame. Arnold suspected that it was Rick Rheingold whom Hadley saw each day when he looked into that enormous rococo mirror in the black-and-gold bathroom, and he was more than a little chagrined when Rick outlived the demise of A. A. Carruthers.

Arnold drank his Scotch as he read Hadley's manuscript. He had to admit it was not badly done. Highly derivative, of course. By Erle Stanley Gardner out of Ross Macdonald. Still, Hadley's style was improving. Arnold read fifty-three pages and was just finishing his second Scotch when Hadley called him to the table. Dinner was steak with beárnaise sauce and a soufflé of mushrooms and fresh spinach. Had he been less hungry Arnold would still have found it delicious. There was no question that Hadley had the touch when it came to food. The red wine that accompanied the meal tasted to Arnold, who had no great palate, very smooth and expensive.

As they ate they discussed Arnold's situation.

"The police do have a point, you know," Hadley said as he refilled Arnold's wine glass. "Why on earth *did* you drive all the way over to Pendleton's. I mean, he's no great buddy of yours, and you had no business to do with him. And to have to borrow a car to get there. You have to admit, Arn, it looks a little fishy."

Come Back, Alice Smythereene! 79

Arnold took a long swallow of wine for fortification, put down his glass and looked directly at Hadley.

"What the police don't know, Had—and what I think Pendleton did—is that I am the real Alice Smythereene."

The effect on Ottinger was remarkable. He dropped the fork from his right hand, sending it clattering against his plate, and stared at Arnold.

"My God!" he exclaimed finally. "Of course! It all makes sense that way. I should have guessed."

Arnold told him almost everything, from the conversation with Herman out of which Alice Smythereene had been born to the phone call from Pendleton informing him of her disappearance. Everything except the story of his disastrous little affair with Sherry. That was too personal; he was not yet ready to talk about it. The telling took more than half an hour, interrupted from time to time by questions from Hadley, who seemed interested in the mechanics of composition—how the ideas had come, how long each book had taken, how many drafts Arnold had written. They finished a bottle of wine and were halfway through a second before Arnold was done with the telling. Then Hadley stared at him in silence for several minutes before asking the next question.

"Who else knows about this?"

"Just you, me, Herman and Elaine. And I'd really like to keep it that way."

Hadley frowned.

"You may have to let the police in on it pretty soon." Then he added, "Well, we can hold off for a while. Let's see what happens."

Together they cleared the table and loaded the dishwasher. Through the kitchen windows Arnold saw that the evening had grown dark. It was time to be getting home. Hadley's thoughts must have been moving in the same direction, for he said, "I guess I'd better drive you home." Then he added, "Hey, I have an idea. Why don't you spend the night here? The guest room is all made up, clean sheets and all. We can sit up for a while and talk, finish that bottle of wine. I have to be at my office early tomorrow. I can get you home before eight."

"Gosh, I don't know. I think maybe I ought to get back. In case Elaine calls."

"Why? Is she away someplace?"

"Elaine's left me, Had."

Once again Hadley was stunned.

"No! I don't believe it. It's not possible. What on earth happened?"

Might as well spill it all, thought Arnold.

"She caught me in bed with Sherry Windsor."

Ottinger stared in disbelief. After a moment's silence a grin spread across his face.

"Why you sly devil! I didn't think you had it in you."

As soon as the words were out Hadley's attitude changed. The grin vanished; a solemn expression clouded his face. His voice dropped in pitch.

"Oh, God! What am I saying? It's terrible. I never would have believed it. You and Elaine—it just doesn't seem possible. I mean, myself . . . well, even back at Yale I sort of knew that I wasn't cut out for steady companionship through life. But you and Elaine were like a rock to me. Like one person. It doesn't seem possible."

Arnold was surprised to see him so moved, and he began to ponder how lonely Hadley must be. The bearnaise sauce, the Chateau Rothschild wine, the sleek Porsche, the beautifully tailored black topcoat with its velvet lapels were part of a disguise, a personality erected piece by piece like a barricade against loneliness.

In the end he decided to stay. It would be too late, anyway, by the time they got back to the city, to expect a call from Elaine. They finished the wine, then retired to the den and drank Scotch, at times talking, at others companionably silent. By the time he went to bed Arnold felt closer to his friend than he had in many years. He also felt blissfully drunk.

Hadley dropped him off in front of his apartment house at seven-thirty the next morning, promising to call later in the day with whatever information he could garner about Pendleton's death and its ramifications. Arnold walked unsmiling past the unctuous Roger, not responding to his "Good Morning, Mr. Simon." He was still smarting over the doorman's betrayal, his too eager cooperation with the police. Besides, he was slightly hung over and in no mood for pleasantries.

As he rode up the elevator Arnold suddenly remembered Francine. The unforeseen rush of yesterday's events had swept away his plan to stop at Milt's Grill and ask about her. That would have to be attended to this morning. He walked out of the elevator and down the hallway to his apartment thinking about the day's schedule. A class at eleven was the first obligatory item. Perhaps it would be better to go to Milt's after that. At the moment he needed a nap. His head ached from too much drink and too little sleep the night before. He wondered at Hadley's ability to rise up cheerfully after such a night and sail wide-eyed straight into the face of the day.

The first sight that caught his eye as he stepped inside the apartment was the mass of books strewn wildly around the living-room floor. The bookcases had been virtually stripped. The drawers of the sideboard had been pulled out and emptied and were lying upside down on the floor. In the bedroom, clothes were everywhere. The closets, the dressers, all had been emptied of their contents, which now lay in every part of the room. The mattress had been pulled from the bed and lay on top of a heap of clothes on the floor.

There was no question about it. The place had been ransacked.

Chapter 10

Roger, of course, knew nothing. He had not even been on duty the previous day. And Walter, his regular replacement, had been sick. A temporary employee had been hired from an agency, but Arnold would have to check with the company that managed the building for details.

He wondered if he should notify the police. His recent encounter with them had not left him much confidence in their goodwill toward him, and he did not look forward to another session of poetry recitation by Farner. On the other hand, it seemed unlikely that the same unit would be involved. Surely the matter would be handled at the local precinct level. He telephoned Hadley's office in search of advice, but the attorney was in conference.

Mrs. Boggs, when she arrived for her weekly cleaning session, took no pains to mask her displeasure.

"It's too much, Mr. Simon. You've gone too far. Just because I get sick and miss a week is no reason to let the place get into this state. I'm surprised at your missus."

Arnold suspected that she drank, and that her failure to appear the previous Wednesday had been the result of a binge rather than illness. For several months he had noticed a depletion of their liquor supply but had said nothing about it. Cleaning women were not so easy to find.

"Mrs. Simon hasn't been around for a while," he told her.

Mrs. Boggs sniffed loudly.

"On vacation or left you?" She fixed an appraising eye on Arnold as if to determine if such a man was worth staying with. "Well, that's her business. I ain't judgin' the right or wrong of it. But you can't let everything slide like this. Even a man living alone got to preserve some standards of decency."

Decency, in Mrs. Boggs's eyes, did not encompass allowing one's apartment to be burglarized. Just as decent men did not give their wives cause to leave them. Arnold tried to temper her indignation with the suggestion of a bonus to be paid for the extra work.

"It ain't a question of money," she answered. "That ain't the point. It's the principle."

She pronounced the last word slowly and carefully as though it were not likely to be found in Arnold's everyday vocabulary. Nevertheless, the promise of pecuniary reward must have mollified her sense of moral outrage, for she set to work putting the living room to rights. As she did so Arnold attempted to compile an inventory of missing items. Not much seemed to have been taken. About a hundred dollars in cash had been removed from a drawer of his desk. He could not remember the exact amount he had kept on hand and felt abashed at having left that much cash in a desk drawer. Elaine's jewelry lay scattered on the floor in front of her dressing table, but it was impossible to tell just what was missing. He picked the pieces up one at a time and returned them to the large leather box in which they were kept, recognizing a few items of sentimental interest as he did so. Elaine had never gone in for expensive jewelry, however, and if anything had been taken the loss could not have amounted to much. The television set and the stereo equipment appeared to be untouched, and Arnold's Hasselblad camera, his fortieth-birthday gift from Elaine, lay in its place on the shelf of the closet. The conclusion Arnold drew from his hasty survey, then, was that except for the cash nothing had been taken. The inescapable suggestion was that the intruder had been after something other than material goods.

Hadley returned Arnold's call after an hour. He was startled by the news of the break-in, and seemed contrite at having kept Arnold away form his apartment the night before.

"I know it's foolish, but I can't help feeling that if I hadn't talked you into staying at my place last night the whole thing might not have happened. I really feel . . ."

He stopped suddenly as though struck by a new thought. Then he resumed in a more somber tone.

"On the other hand, Arn, if nothing much is missing—I mean if it wasn't just an ordinary burglary, then maybe it's just as well you weren't there. I mean maybe it was . . ."

He let his voice trail off, unwilling to complete the sentence. Arnold finished it for him.

"Maybe it was *me* they were after."

The idea had occurred to him earlier, during his inspection of the apartment. But now that he said it aloud it frightened him. It seemed especially ominous in light of the bombing of Francine's car.

Hadley changed the subject. He had other information to impart, having already done some investigation on Arnold's behalf.

"Augie Mancuso," he told Arnold, "is a Mafia captain in northern New Jersey. From what I could find out, Matt Pendleton had dealings with him back in the days when he was still Mario Parente. I don't know whether they kept up the association. And Vinnie Viola is a second-rate racketeer operating in Lower Manhattan. Hookers and drugs, mostly. Nobody I talked to knew anything for certain, but it seems there's bad blood between Mancuso and Viola. Apparently they were buddies a few years back, but lately Mancuso has been trying to set up shop in Manhattan, and there could be a gang war brewing. Pendleton may have been the first casualty. Arnie, I think you may have got yourself caught in the middle of some bad business."

"A gang war?" Arnold was aghast. "What the hell have I got to do with a gang war?"

"I guess that's what the police are wondering. Special unit number three, by the way, is a task force assigned to investigate Mafia drug dealings in Lower Manhattan."

Hadley paused to clear his throat. When he resumed his voice had a more businesslike tone.

"Arnold, I have to ask you something. First let me assure you that I'll be glad to represent you no matter what you've done, but it's important that I know the whole story. Are you mixed up in something illicit?"

"Hadley, are you crazy? What the hell would I know about anything illicit? The last illicit thing I was mixed up in was thirty years ago when my cousin Melvin and I swiped a box of bubble-gum cards from Brodsky's candy store. And then I was so nervous about it I had bad dreams for a week that old lady Brodsky was chasing me."

"All right, Arnold. Don't get so worked up. I had to ask."

"Hadley, all I know is that somebody's doing a number on me and I don't know why."

Hadley's voice became professionally reassuring.

"I don't want you to worry, Arnold. I'm sure we'll get everything straightened out."

"Yeah, sure." Arnold was unconvinced. "If nobody blows me up or stabs me to death in my sleep, maybe you can keep me out of jail."

"Oh, come on, Arnold. Don't be melodramatic. I'm

sure there's a rational explanation for everything that's been going on. And we'll find it. A case of mistaken identity, probably. In the meantime, though, I think the police are going to want to talk to you, and I think it would be a good idea for us to get together first. Let's see."

There was a pause, presumably to let Hadley consult his engagement calendar.

"Are you free for dinner this evening?"

"If I'm still alive."

Hadley ignored Arnold's churlishness.

"Let's say seven o'clock at La Fenice on MacDougal Street. They make the loveliest *fettucine alla vongole* you ever tasted. I'll have my secretary make the reservation. Okay?"

"Okay. What about the break-in? Do I report it?"

Hadley thought for a moment.

"Report it to your local precinct. They'll send someone round to investigate. But I don't want you talking to those special unit boys unless I'm present. That's a must."

Then as an afterthought he added, "Oh, by the way, I never did get to ask you what you thought of my manuscript."

Arnold rolled his eyes heavenward. God save us from writers and their egos, he thought.

"It was fine, Had."

"Yeah. Ol' Rick Rheingold still has a few stories left in him, don't you think?"

Arnold wondered if he was being charged for the conversation.

The plainclothesman who came in answer to his call to the precinct was young, almost young enough in looks to be one of Arnold's students. And to Arnold's annoyance he treated him with the deference usually accorded a much older person. Being forty was depressing enough, it seemed to him, without policemen treating him like an elder. Perhaps it was time to change his hairstyle or abandon his conventional tweeds for a more flamboyant mode of dress.

The interview did not last long. The policeman filled out a two-page form and promised to get in touch if there were anything to report. But he did not hold out much hope.

"With nothing missing but cash it's not likely anything will turn up." He shook his head. "It's one helluva strange burglary."

Arnold did not volunteer any information on that score.

"Well, Mr. Simon, I guess that's it. Sorry I can't do anything more for you. I realize what a shock this kind of thing can be. We'll be in touch."

After he left, Arnold telephoned Elaine's clinic. The receptionist put him through to Beverly.

"Sorry, Arn, but Elaine is out on a case. Not that I can guarantee she'd talk to you if she was here. Look, why don't you give her another day or so to cool off. Call her tomorrow. I think she'll talk to you by then."

Cold comfort from every quarter, thought Arnold.

Luther Washington was waiting for him at his office after class. It was a quarter past twelve when Arnold got there, and as he walked past the desk of old Mrs. Donovan, the department secretary jerked her head in the direction of his office.

"An old friend of ours is here to see you. I let him wait in your office."

Then she rolled her eyes and added, *"Très distingué."*

Luther had grown a beard since Arnold had last seen him, of medium length and neatly trimmed. He wore a dark gray three-piece suit, and on his head sat a pale lavender turban with a large imitation ruby in the center, just above his forehead. Together with the light-chocolate color of his face, the outfit bespoke an Indian of the higher castes, a diplomat, perhaps. Arnold stared at him.

"Amazing," he said.

"You like the effect?"

"I thought you gurus specialized in scraggly gray beards and long dirty white gowns."

"Not nowadays. What you have is an outdated picture. Today's minister of Vishnu is modern. Up-to-date in dress and manner. Inspires confidence."

"Sort of an Eastern Jerry Falwell?"

"I would have preferred Billy Graham. But basically correct. The scene has changed, man, away from grubby adolescents. Poor little rich kids ain't where it's at. Today's seeker is older, you know? Looking for something more solid—a spiritual investment banker."

Luther looked at his watch.

"As a matter of fact, you're late, dad. I have an appointment uptown at two o'clock with a soul in need of guidance. Up at her place on Madison and Eighty-first."

"Late for what?"

Luther looked hurt.

"Aw shit, man, you forgot. We had an appointment for lunch today. To discuss tonight's creative writing awards. The All City Creative Writing Competition, remember? Hell, Arnold, you're a judge. You promised to give a little speech."

Arnold could have kicked himself for forgetting. It was the one thing other than sheer survival that Luther took seriously. Even after the loss of funding he had continued to work with ghetto youths, trying to heighten their awareness of the beauty and power of language and of the force of their own creativity. Every year for the past three or four he had coaxed and prodded a few of his charges into entering the citywide competition, and this year he had worked his way onto the organizing committee. It was the first time Arnold had been asked to judge, and he suspected it had been engineered by Luther with an eye to giving his protégés an edge.

"I'm sorry, Luther. I forgot our lunch date. I've been

under a lot of strain." He reached into the lower left-hand drawer of his desk and pulled out two file folders. "But I didn't forget about the contest."

It was true. Arnold had received the packet of poems and stories, those that had survived the initial winnowing process, two weeks earlier, and had spent several hours studying them.

"I thought one of your kids' poems was pretty good, actually. The one about finding the dead pigeon on Atlantic Avenue." He leafed through the folders. "Here it is. Clifford Johnson."

Luther brightened considerably.

"Yeah. That kid's got something. If only I can poke a hole in his defenses big enough to let it out."

He clapped his hands.

"Well, Vishnu bless you, sahib. And here I was thinking nobody knows you when you're down and out. Come on. Just to show there's no hard feelings, I'll let you buy me lunch."

As they walked up Mercer toward Eighth Street, Luther discoursed on the subject of his appointment later that afternoon.

"Sordid little story of our time, you know. Husband made a small fortune manufacturing plastic margarine tubs, then ran off with his twenty-two-year-old secretary. Leaving a poor woman in need of spiritual comfort."

"Which is where you come in," said Arnold. "To the rescue, looking like the Aga Khan in your three-piece suit and turban."

"The poor soul needs guidancce. Someone she can trust, relate to."

"Don't you think your new image is a little incompatible with a storefront on St. Mark's Place?"

"Hey, man, what do you want? Even the Reverend Moon had to start somewhere. Besides, you've hit on one of the main agenda items for today's meeting with my benefactress-to-be. My lease is up at the end of the month, and I'm hoping to move into more suitable surroundings. Nothing open in your building, I suppose?"

Arnold laughed and shook his head.

"'Well! Some people talk of morality, and some of religion, but give me a little snug property.' Do you know that quote?"

"Jane Austen?" Luther ventured.

"Not a bad guess. Maria Edgeworth, actually."

They had turned up Eighth Street and were now in front of Milt's Grill. Arnold pulled open the door and let Luther precede him inside. The place was crowded; it was the height of the lunch hour. Arnold spied Francine at the other end of the room removing dirty dishes from a freshly vacated table. He was surprised to see her back to work so soon. It occurred to him for the first time that she probably could not afford to lose another day's pay.

Milt was in his usual place behind the cash register, engaged in a whispered conversation with Iris. As he spoke he pointed toward Arnold and Luther. Then, yielding his place to Iris, he squeezed his way across the crowded room to where they stood waiting for a table.

"Hey, Perfesser. How ya been," he said when he reached them. Then in a lower tone he added, "Hey, Perfesser, I don't want no trouble in here. I mean, nothing's gonna happen, right? I'm just tryin' to run a luncheonette. I don't want no trouble."

Under Arnold's incredulous stare he felt the need to expand.

"I mean, first with Francine's car. Then the cops comin' in askin' about you. It's just that I . . ."

"The police were in here? Asking about me?"

"Yesterday morning. They wanted to know all about you. How often did you come in here, was you alone or with people, what was up between you and Francine, you know?"

Then he hastily added, "I didn't tell 'em nothing."

Luther looked at Arnold questioningly.

"I didn't know you were a man of mystery, sahib."

From the register Iris was calling, "Hey, Milt! I gotta get back to the counter." A few people in their immediate vicinity turned to glance at the three men. Arnold felt the need to produce something by way of explanation.

"I can't talk about it here, Milt," he said in an exaggerated whisper. "It's secret business."

He held one finger close to Milt, shielded it with his other hand from the eyes of nearby patrons, and wrote the letters C I A in the air. Milt eyed him suspiciously.

"I gotta get back to the register," he said. "Why don't you take that booth all the way in the back, the one Francine just cleared off. I just don't want no trouble."

He walked back to his place at the register, mumbling to himself as he went.

"What was that all about?" Luther wanted to know when they had seated themselves. Before Arnold could answer, Francine appeared with two glasses of water.

"Hello, Arnold"

All in all, she did not look too bad. A slight blackening of the right eye and a strip of gauze taped just below the left. There were also several burn marks along her forearms. He wished he had sent her flowers.

"Francine, I'm sorry. I had no idea anything like that would happen. I just don't know what to say."

She looked at him nervously.

"I guess it's not your fault. I just hope you're not mixed up in something bad."

"Mixed up in something bad?" interrupted Luther. "Man, you're deeper than I thought."

Francine turned and stared at Luther as though she had just become aware of him. She gazed intently at the light-brown face capped by the lavender turban with its garish red jewel.

"Oh, Francine," said Arnold. "This is my friend . . ."

"Lodha Vishnu Dan," interjected Luther. "Minister of Vishnu. My card."

He took a small leather case from his breast pocket and extracted a business card which he handed to Francine. She glanced at it briefly, then resumed staring at Luther.

"Lodha," she murmured. "What a lovely name."

Luther pressed his palms together and inclined his head forward.

"Om Vishnu Vishnaya," he said.

"How beautiful," cooed Francine. "What does it mean?"

"It means," said Arnold, "never give a follower of Vishnu an even break."

Francine glared at him, then turned to Luther and smiled sweetly.

"It must be wonderful being a minister. Spiritual, I mean. I think spiritual things are wonderful."

"Yeah, well right now I'm interested in something temporal," said Arnold. "Like a B.L.T. on toast with a side of french fries."

"Forgive him, O flower of Vishnu," Luther told the girl, reaching out to touch her cheek lightly. "He does not share our love of the spirit."

Luther's love of the spirit did not stop him from ordering a double steak sandwich, french fries and a chocolate malted. When Francine had gone to fetch their order Arnold chided him.

"Don't you think you were laying it on a little thick for that poor girl? I mean, she doesn't have any money to donate to the temple."

Luther looked indignant.

"Do you think I care only for money? That young woman glows with an inner beauty. And the shell's not half bad, either."

"Luther, lay off her. I don't want her to get hurt."

"Vishnu heals, never hurts, sahib. Now tell me about your little mystery."

Arnold recited his story again while they ate, starting with the phone call from Pendleton four days before and ending with the ransacking of his apartment, but withholding any mention of Sherry Windsor or Alice Smythereene. When he finished Luther released a long whistle.

"Whew! It sounds like you're in some mess, man. What's behind it?"

"Damned if I know. That's what really scares me. I have no idea what's going on."

Luther was silent for a few moments. Then he said, "I have a friend in the police department. He was sort of my parole officer way back when. Works out of headquarters now. I could ask him to find out what's going on."

"Gee, I don't know." Arnold wondered what Hadley Ottinger would think of that. "Well, I guess it can't hurt."

"Come to think of it, I'm seeing him tonight. He's giving me a ride up to LaGuardia High School. Do you want to ride with us? That way you can tell him the story yourself."

"Where's LaGuardia High School?"

Luther stared at him.

"On Amsterdam Avenue, behind Lincoln Center." Then, in response to Arnold's puzzled air, he added, "Where the creative writing awards are being handed out tonight. Or have you forgotten already?"

"Oh, of course."

"Well, since you're going too, why don't you ride up there with us? That way you can tell him the story yourself."

Arnold did, in fact, need a ride. Elaine still had the car, and the subway journey was not a cheering prospect.

He agreed to let Luther pick him up in front of his apartment building at seven-fifteen that evening.

Francine hovered about their table throughout lunch like a mother bird about her nest. Had Luther sat with open mouth and outstretched neck, Arnold was sure she would have been happy to feed him. He was disappointed by her fickleness.

"About the car," he told Francine as they were leaving. "I feel I should replace it. Why don't you look around for one and let me know what it costs."

"And I, my Vishnu flower," said Luther, "would like to comfort you for the trials you have undergone."

Francine smiled at him.

"Have a nice day, Lodha." Then, as an afterthought, she added, "You, too, Arnold."

Outside the restaurant they parted, Arnold to Fifth Avenue, Luther toward Broadway.

"Good luck with your patroness. I still think you ought to concentrate your attention in that part of town and leave these poor little Village girls alone."

"From each according to her ability, sahib. To each according to her need. See you at seven-fifteen, *n'est-ce-pas?*"

"Yeah, fine. Thanks."

"My pleasure, sahib."

He put his palms together in front of his chest, fingers pointing upward, and made a slight bow. Then he straightened, smiled at Arnold and lifted two fingers to his temple in salute.

"Uptown, Vishnu soldiers," he said. Then he turned and glided regally down the street.

Chapter 11

Arnold spent the afternoon working on that evening's speech and correcting proofs of an article on Rudyard Kipling he had written for the *Journal of Victorian Literature*. It was not until four o'clock that he remembered his dinner engagement with Hadley Ottinger. It would have to be put off. He telephoned the lawyer's office, but Hadley was in conference and could not come to the phone.

"Could you please give him the message that Mr. Simon—uh, Professor Simon, that is—can't meet him for dinner tonight?" Arnold felt a cowardly sense of relief at not having to give Hadley the news in person. "I'll call him tomorrow to arrange another appointment."

His relief was short-lived, for Hadley returned his call in less than fifteen minutes.

"Arnold, what do you mean you can't meet me for dinner tonight? I passed up a chance to dine with Lawrence Vandewalle for you. He's up for an appellate court judgeship. That's how important I think it is for us to get together as soon as possible. What could be so pressing as to keep you away?"

Arnold told him of his committment to the All City Creative Writing Awards. To Hadley the weight of such an engagement was negligible when put in the scale against, say, dinner with a future appellate court judge.

"Really, Arnold, your sense of priorities amazes me. Perhaps you don't realize how serious your situation may be vis-à-vis the police."

"But I haven't done anything," Arnold protested.

"That's hardly the point. They're going to ask you some hard questions, and, guilty or innocent, you'd better be ready with the answers. However, if you think it's more important to spend the evening patting the acned cheeks of a roomful of would-be Tennysons, I guess there's precious little I can do about it."

"It's just that I can't let Luther Washington down. It's very important to him."

"Well, I suppose I can call Vandewalle back and see if he's still free. All right, let's see. Tomorrow's Thursday—that's no good. I'll be in court all morning, then I have a golfing date with Wyatt McKenzie in the afternoon. Do you know him? He's about to become Assistant Attorney General."

Arnold had to admit he did not know Wyatt McKenzie, just as he did not know Lawrence Vandewalle and the myriad of other up-and-coming movers and shakers with whom Hadley socialized.

"Well, how's Friday for lunch? One o'clock."

Arnold paused long enough to give the impression of consulting a date book.

"That's fine, Had."

"Okay. One o'clock, then. Although I find their lunches fall rather short of their dinners. Still, they make a rather tasty *tortellini in brodo*."

"Okay. One o'clock it is. Do you want me to make reservations?"

"No. I'll have my secretary do it when she cancels tonight's. Well, I'm off then. See you Friday."

Off where, Arnold wondered. Racquet ball with the

Come Back, Alice Smythereene! 97

next governor, probably. Or tea with the future ambassador to Nepal.

Arnold was waiting outside his apartment building at seven-fifteen that evening when the small blue Honda pulled up to the curb in front of him. Luther got out of the two-door car to allow Arnold to enter the back. He was still wearing the three-piece suit but had abandoned the turban. As Arnold squeezed into the automobile he saw to his astonishment that the driver was none other than Detective Sergeant Henry Farner.

"Hello there, Professor Simon," said the big policeman cheerfully. "You seem surprised to see me."

Surprised hardly expressed the shock Arnold experienced at seeing the detective.

"My God! I didn't know you two knew one another."

Farner chuckled, evidently pleased with the effect his presence had produced.

"Oh yes, indeed. We've known each other for a very long time. Let's see—how long has it been?" he asked Luther.

"About a hundred years, pops," Luther replied. He seemed less eager than the detective to revive past memories.

"I guess it must be over ten years now," Farner went on, answering his own question. "I was working out of Brooklyn then. Central juvenile division. And this young man was working hard—very hard—at becoming a criminal. But there was something about him—sensitivity, maybe, or a gift for words. So after his conviction I kept in touch with him and persuaded him to enroll in your program, Professor. I just knew he had it in him to do something worthwhile."

"Ah, come off it, man," said Luther uncomfortably.

"No. I want that young boy back there to hear what I'm saying."

Farner's reference was to the fourth occupant of the car, a boy about fourteen years old who was sharing the tiny back seat with Arnold. The boy looked warily around him and said nothing.

"Arnold, this is Clifford Johnson," said Luther. "Clifford, this is Mr. Simon. He's a friend of mine and a big-time professor and poet. He's also one of the judges of the contest, and he liked your poem."

Clifford remained impassive. Arnold murmured a greeting and a terse remark in praise of Clifford's literary effort. He felt slightly uncomfortable because he had awarded it only a second-place vote.

"Some of us get the chance to do what the rest of us only dream of doing," Farner went on as though there had been no interruption. "If you have the talent and the nerve and the luck to become something better than you are. Maybe I just wanted some vicarious satisfaction out of someone else's success. But when that book of poetry was published and Luther Washington got all those accolades, well I . . ."

He paused, searching for words.

"Ah, pops. Let it drop," said Luther. But Farner was determined to continue.

"It's just a shame to see someone with all that talent let it go to waste for a bunch of foolishness."

There was an uncomfortable silence as Farner returned his full attention to the road while Luther turned his head away and stared out the side window. Scrunched up in the tiny back seat, his knees pushing into his stomach, Arnold almost wished he had taken his chances with the subway. He recalled his conversation earlier in the day with Luther and the latter's appointment with a potential patroness.

"How did things go uptown today?" he asked.

"I'll tell you about it later, man."

Luther was obviously reluctant to discuss the matter

in front of Farner. From the opposite corner of the back seat Clifford spoke up for the first time.

"It's between him and some born-again Christian dude. Luther says he's better lookin', but the other guy got the edge 'cause he's white."

Farner found a parking space on West End Avenue below Sixty-fourth Street. As they walked toward the high school the detective placed a restraining hand on Arnold's arm and said in a low voice, "If you don't mind, Professor. Why don't we let Luther and Clifford walk ahead a bit. I'd like to have a few words with you." To the others he added in a louder tone. "You two go on ahead. We'll catch up in a few minutes."

Gone was the avuncular tone he had adopted in the car. Farner again loomed in Arnold's eyes as a detective with the special unit number three.

"This probably isn't the time or place to discuss it, Professor, but I can't let the opportunity pass to tell you what a big mistake it is to hold back information. Whatever you've done, whatever kind of trouble you're in, you'd be much better off cooperating with us. We'll help you in any way we can if you'll just come clean with us."

Arnold replied in a voice that betrayed his agitation.

"Look, Sergeant Farner, there's nothing to come clean about. I haven't done anything. I'm just an innocent victim in all of this."

He was about to tell Farner about the break-in of his apartment when he recalled Hadley's warning about talking to members of the special unit.

"Anyway," he added, "my lawyer has advised me not to talk to you fellows without him present."

Farner started to say something, then changed his mind. They walked the remaining half block in silence.

The others were waiting at the top of the steps just in

front of the school entrance. Luther was talking to a short, bald man in a plaid sports jacket.

"You're third on the program," Luther said as they came up. "This is Herb Sims, chairman of the committee."

Sims extended his hand. "It's a pleasure to meet you, Professor Simon. I'm looking forward to your presentation."

"My speech!" cried Arnold as they shook hands.

Sims gave him a puzzled look.

"My speech. I left it in the car."

He had carried it in a plastic portfolio along with a sheaf of poems he was to judge and his notes on them. He must have left it on the back window shelf.

"I'll run back and get it. It'll only take a few minutes."

Before anyone could reply he ran down the steps to the street.

"I'll meet you inside," he called back over his shoulder.

He was glad to be alone, free of Farner's company for a moment. He hurried to the corner and turned right into Sixty-fourth Street.

As he walked the long block toward West End Avenue he had the sensation of being followed. A car was moving in the street to his left, hugging the row of cars parked along the curb, keeping pace with him as he moved along. He could see the front end out of the corner of his eye, large yellow hood and fenders just in back of him, following close behind.

He quickened his steps, then broke into a trot. The car stayed with him. Halfway down the block he stopped. The car moved ahead and stopped twenty feet up the street. It was a large yellow Buick.

A large yellow Buick had followed him from Pendleton's house the previous Saturday.

He stood still, looking up and down the street. A young, well-dressed couple who had passed him moments earlier were part way down the block toward Amsterdam, holding hands and singing as they walked jauntily away. Across the street two men in undershirts stood in a doorway talking quietly. Further down in the direction of West End a group of kids was gathered around a parked car, pushing and shoving and laughing uproariously.

I'm being ridiculous, he thought. There must be a thousand large yellow Buicks in New York. But there it stood twenty feet away, waiting for him to make his move.

He crossed the street and headed for the men in undershirts.

"Uh, excuse me. Do you know what time it is?"

One of the men shrugged and held up his wrists to show he had no watch. The other did not look at him.

"Nice evening, isn't it?"

"You want something?" It was the second man who spoke.

"Uh, no. Not especially."

"Then why don't you use your own watch?"

He pointed to Arnold's wrist watch showing just below the sleeve.

"Oh." Arnold smiled weakly. "I wasn't sure if it was right."

It showed five minutes to eight. If he did not hurry he would be late for his speech.

He looked up the street. The car was gone.

The events of recent days had his nerves on edge, he told himself. He couldn't allow himself to be menaced by every yellow Buick driving the streets of Manhattan. Besides, he wasn't even sure the car he had seen last Saturday had been following him.

He walked quickly up the street, and, as he waited at the corner for the light to turn green, looked nervously up and down West End Avenue for the yellow Buick. It was not in sight. Arnold crossed to the other side and turned south to where Farner's car was parked half a block below. As he approached it he saw his plastic portfolio sitting on the rear window ledge. He jogged the last few steps to the Honda, bent down and grasped the handle of the passenger door. There was no response to his pressure on the latch. The car was locked. He had forgotten to take the keys.

He remained for a moment in a stooped position at the door of the car, peering at the portfolio inside and cursing himself for an absent-minded idiot. Then he straightened up and looked over the roof of Farner's car.

The big yellow Buick was standing on the other side.

He stared at it, unable to move. His mouth was dry, and a sick feeling began to radiate from the pit of his stomach.

The door of the Buick opened and the driver got out. He looked directly at Arnold, his mouth curved in a tight-lipped smile. Even in the dim half-light there was no mistaking the features.

Over the big, bulbous nose the eyes were narrowed to slits as they stared at him.

Arnold looked wildly around, up and down the street. The traffic on West End was light at that hour, a scattering of motorists speeding heedlessly by. At his back was a high cyclone fence, and behind it several rows of delivery trucks stood empty and locked up for the night. Across the street a row of dingy commercial buildings showed no sign of life. Farther down the block on that side, almost at the corner, a small cluster of people stood around the entrance to a high-rise apartment project, too far away to be of much help.

In the other direction, at the corner of Sixty-fourth Street, a few people waited to cross West End. His best hope, he decided, lay that way.

The man had come around the front of the Buick and was edging between two parked cars. As he stepped up onto the sidewalk Arnold broke and ran north toward Sixty-fourth, shouting as he went.

"Help!"

The people at the corner were already crossing the street. No one seemed to hear him. He glanced back over his shoulder. The figure behind him was gaining ground.

"Help! Somebody!"

His legs buckled and he fell to the sidewalk.

"Help!" It came out more as a whimper than a cry.

"Hey! What's going on there? Simon, is that you?"

It was Farner's voice! Raising his head Arnold saw the tall form of the detective running down the street in his direction on the other side of the row of parked cars.

"Farner! It's him!"

"Halt!"

The big detective thundered past. In his left hand was a gun, muzzle pointed upward.

"Halt or I'll fire!"

Arnold saw his pursuer beating a quick retreat to the waiting Buick. Just as Farner reached it its engine turned over and it began to move forward. He tried to keep abreast, making a lunge for the door handle, but the car picked up speed and roared away, sending Farner sprawling to the gutter.

There was a squeal of tires as a taxi skidded to a stop a few feet behind the prone figure of the detective. The driver leaned out the window.

"For Christ's sake, buddy! Why don't you look where you're going?"

As Arnold limped toward the scene he saw the detective rise to his knees and remain in that position for a moment rubbing his head.

"You all right, mac?" shouted the taxi driver.

Farner got slowly to his feet and made his way to the

curb. Without waiting for any further answer the taxi drove away. By the time Arnold reached him the detective had gained the sidewalk and was leaning against a parked car.

"Farner. Are you all right?"

The detective was breathing hard and waited a few seconds before answering.

"I've been better," he finally replied. "But nothing broken. Just knocked the wind out of me a bit. How about you?"

Arnold noticed that his pants were torn and his knee was bleeding. It was the same leg he had injured at Pendleton's house four days earlier.

"I'm okay," he said.

Farner smiled wryly at him.

"You forgot the car keys, Professor."

"I know. It's a good thing I did, I guess. Otherwise . . ."

They stood in silence for several moments before Arnold spoke again.

"Sergeant, that man. It's the same one. The one I saw in Pendleton's backyard."

Farner looked at him a few seconds before replying. Then he said, "Well, at least I got his license number."

Chapter 12

They formed a somber little group on the way home. Clifford, who had not won a prize despite a second-place vote from Arnold, was even more withdrawn than on the trip uptown, and sat silently clutching his certificate of participation. Luther was even more upset. After some initial remarks on the narrow pedantry of the judges—a denunciation from which he took no pains to exclude Arnold—he lapsed into silence. Farner, for his part, stared thoughtfully through the windshield in front of him.

Arnold had insisted, against Farner's advice, on going through with his part of the program. He and Farner had finally arrived nearly half an hour late, both with torn clothing, and Arnold with a wet handkerchief tied around his bleeding knee. He had given his little speech and helped pass out the awards with full concentration on the task at hand. Now that it was over he felt tired and frightened. He began to shiver.

"Could you turn the heat up a little?" he asked.

"Feeling chilled?"

Farner eased the car to the curb and left the engine running. Then he addressed Luther.

"There's a bottle in the glove compartment. Why don't you reach in and get it and pass it around."

Luther withdrew a pint bottle of Jack Daniels and unscrewed the cap. After taking a swallow he passed it back to Arnold.

"I keep it to ward off chills," said Farner as Arnold drank from the bottle. "That and snake bite, you might say. Occupational hazards."

He chuckled and accepted the pint of bourbon from Arnold. Clifford spoke for the first time since getting into the car.

"Can I have some, too?"

"Indeed not," Farner replied.

"Shee-ut. I done drunk plenty of that stuff before."

Farner turned around and eyed Clifford sternly. He loomed very large over the seat.

"The word is *shit*, not *shee-ut*. One syllable. If you choose to use profanity, at least pronounce the words correctly. And saying 'I done drunk' makes you sound ignorant. You know better than that. Now as far as drinking is concerned, you are under the legal age by quite a few years. If you think that drinking bourbon makes you a big man, then you've got a lot to learn. At any rate, you're not going to drink any in my car."

He turned back and put the car in gear. Arnold glanced at Clifford, whose face was set in an attitude halfway between sullenness and tears.

"Hey, Clifford," he said to him, "I have some friends who edit college poetry magazines. I think your poem might be good enough to get published in one of them. Anyway, I'd like to try. Would that be okay with you?"

The boy was silent. Luther spoke up quietly.

"Answer the man, Clifford."

"Yeah," responded Clifford.

"Yeah, what?" Luther prodded.

After a few moments of silence Clifford added, "Yeah, that's okay with me."

Luther let the matter drop and they rode on in si-

Come Back, Alice Smythereene! 107

lence. Maybe, thought Arnold, with hard work and encouragement and luck Clifford might indeed be a published poet some day. Operating a fake Hindu church out of a store front, perhaps. Or writing historical romances under a pseudonym, with someone trying to murder him.

To Arnold's surprise Farner took them to police headquarters. As he parked the car he said to Luther, "What I'd like you to do is take Clifford home, then come back here and pick us up." Then to Arnold he added, "Professor, I know it's been a tough evening, but if you can bring yourself to do it, I'd like you to look through some photographs to see if you can identify that man. I'd like you to do it now, if possible, while his face is still fresh in your mind."

"I don't think I'm ever likely to forget that face," Arnold replied. He longed to be at home in bed, covers drawn tightly around him. The chills had returned. On the other hand he felt a certain safety in Farner's presence which he was loathe to relinquish.

"All right," he said. "We may as well do it now."

They entered the building together. Farner led him to a room on the second floor.

"Have a seat in here, Professor. I'll be right back."

He returned in less than five minutes with a mug of black coffee and two thick books of photographs.

"I'll be in my office, two doors to the left down the hall. Just call out when you spot him. Oh, and there's more coffee in the squad room. At the end of the hall to the right. Just tell them I sent you. In the meantime, I'm going to try and get through some paperwork."

The room was a small one, some sort of conference room it seemed to Arnold, with nothing but a single long table and ten chairs. It was brilliantly lighted by an overhead bank of flourescent tubes. Arnold sat at the head of the table and went painstakingly through the first book, looking carefully at every photograph. It took the better part of an hour, during which Luther returned and sat down facing him at the opposite end of the table. The image of the two of them seated at opposite ends of the ten-foot table registered in Arnold's mind like a scene in a movie—an eccentric dinner party for two in some English baronial manor—and he half expected Farner to enter bearing a silver chafing dish. He was, he decided, verging on hysteria. His energy had ebbed, and he was beginning to shiver.

"Hey, man, you all right?" Luther asked him solicitously. "You're looking kind of sick."

"I don't feel so good," replied Arnold, turning the pages of the photograph book in a desultory manner as he spoke.

Then all at once he saw it.

"Good God, I've found it!" he exclaimed.

The bulbous nose, the deep-set eyes, the dull, mean face stared up at him from the photograph on the table.

"I'll get Henry," said Luther.

He returned immediately with the detective, who studied the picture and the file card attached to it.

"The name is Lenny Manuszak. Thirty-six-year-old male. Caucasian, six foot one, two hundred and fifteen pounds. Former semi-pro prize fighter, now a small-time hood. Sometimes does muscle work for Augie Mancuso. Five arrests, two convictions. The first for dealing in a controlled substance, the other, more recent, for assault with a deadly weapon. Does any of that ring a bell, Professor? Do you know anything about him?"

Arnold shook his head. His shivering had increased.

"I never saw him before that time in Pendleton's backyard."

"Well, he certainly knows a lot about you. How do you suppose he knows where to find you?"

"Hey, pops," Luther interjected. "The man's not well. Can't you hold the questions for another day?"

"Yes, of course. You're right. Besides, my boss will want to be in on any further questioning. I'm afraid we're going to have to ask you down here again, Professor Simon. But for now Luther's right. We'd better take you home."

"And you'd better get some medication, man," added Luther. "Like a tranquilizer. Better have Elaine call a doctor."

"There is no Elaine, Luther." Arnold had trouble speaking. Luther stared at him. "I mean not at my place. She left me."

Luther was shocked by this latest piece of information.

"Well, I'll be damned," he said. Then to Farner he added, "I don't think he should be left alone. Maybe we ought to check him in someplace where they can keep an eye on him during the night."

Arnold protested.

"Well, then—how about I come home with you," Luther suggested. "Henry can swing by my place to let me pick up a few things, can't you, pops? Then I'll just spend the night as your nurse. I could use a night away from that damned store, anyway."

Arnold nodded in assent. He was tired and ill and would have agreed to almost anything to end the discussion and get started for home. Besides, he had to admit he was a little afraid of going home alone.

Luther made a bed for himself on the couch. Then he brewed some sort of potion, which he insisted on Arnold's drinking before going to bed.

"It isn't any of that god-damned herb tea, is it?" Arnold wanted to know.

"Ah, no, man. Just drink it. It'll help you sleep."

Arnold sniffed at it. It smelled strongly alcoholic.

"What's in it?"

"Eye of newt and toe of frog. Shit, man. Just drink it so we can go to bed."

Arnold closed his eyes and drained the glass. It didn't taste bad.

"Listen, Luther. Er, thanks for staying with me."

"My pleasure, sahib. May Vishnu guard your dreams."

Arnold smiled.

"Good night, Lodha. *Om Vishnu Vishnaya.*"

During the night he was awakened by a noise from the living room. A humming, vibrating sound. An odor, sweet and heavy, reached him. A sense of fear began rising from the pit of his stomach.

He forced himself to get out of bed and walk to the bedroom door slowly, as noiselessly as he could.

"Luther?" he called softly through the door. Too softly to be heard.

"Luther?" he repeated in a louder voice.

No response.

Oh God, he thought. Don't let anything bad have happened.

He opened the door in stages, trying without success to keep it from squeaking. Looking round the corner of the jamb he could make out a low light at the end of the hall. The sound was clearer now.

O-o-o-o-m-m-m-m.

He walked gingerly down the hall to the living room. There on the floor sat Luther, clad in a pair of undershorts, legs folded beneath him. With his hands in an attitude of prayer in front of his chest, he swayed back and forth in time to his chant.

O-o-o-o-m-m-m-m.

Next to Luther on the floor was a saucer in which

stood a smoking miniature brazier. Burning incense, from the smell of it.

"*O-o-o-a-m-m-m-m,*" droned Luther.

Arnold expelled the breath he had been holding.

"Jesus Christ," he swore softly. He stared at the swaying body for a full minute before speaking again.

"Luther, don't tell me you actually believe in that crap."

Without stopping the motion of his body Luther paused in his chanting.

"It doesn't hurt to keep in practice," he answered.

Arnold, dumbfounded, continued to stare.

"Shee-ut!" he exclaimed.

In the morning he awoke to the smell of coffee. The clock on the bedside table indicated ten o'clock.

"I called the university and cancelled your classes for today," Luther told him when he came into the kitchen. "And tomorrow. I figured you could use a couple of days off. How you feeling?"

"Luther, you're amazing. You should have been a nurse."

"Yeah. Lodha the physician." He set a cup of hot coffee in front of Arnold. "I thought maybe we'd just have some coffee and toast, and then go over to Milt's Grill for something more substantial."

Arnold peered at his friend over the rim of his coffee cup.

"Luther, go easy on Francine. She's sort of—vulnerable."

"Shit, man. I thought it was just your sisters y'all didn't want us messin' round with."

"Well, I just don't want her being made a sacrificial virgin to Vishnu."

"You're saving her for the exploding car ceremony,

is that it? Well, don't worry, sahib. We gave up sacrificing virgins a long time ago. Couldn't find any."

The telephone was ringing. Arnold was not sorry for the interruption.

"Good morning, Professor Simon. I hope you're feeling better."

It was Farner.

"A lot better, thanks." Arnold paused, searching for words. "Uh, Sergeant Farner, about last night . . . I was too shaken up to thank you, but I . . . I just want you to know . . ."

Farner cut him off.

"Just doing my job, Professor. Well, I called to tell you I got a make on the car. Thought you might be interested in knowing about it. It's registered to a Herman Charnoff, 2594 Central Park West."

"Oh my God!" said Arnold.

"The name is not unfamiliar, I take it."

"Sergeant Farner, Herman Charnoff is my agent. Er, was my agent. When I was writing thrillers."

"Yes, sir. I have to confess I knew that before I called. I'm also aware that he's the agent of the missing Miss Smythereene."

"Sergeant, what on earth do you suppose that gangster is doing with Herman Charnoff's car?"

"I was hoping *you* could enlighten *us* on that subject, sir."

"Do you know that Herman's out of town?"

"Yes, sir. I got that from his answering service. Do you have any idea where he's gone? Or why?"

"No. Dear God. Do you suppose something has happened to him?"

"I don't know. He sure picked a dandy time to go on vacation. At any rate, Professor, I hope you're not planning on leaving town. My boss, Captain McPartland, would like to talk to you some time soon."

"Look here, Sergeant Farner. Am I under suspicion for something?"

There was a pause, too long for Arnold's comfort, before the detective replied.

"I wouldn't go that far, Professor. But there are sure some things we think you could help us clear up."

"But I don't know anything," Arnold insisted.

"If you'll pardon my saying so, I think you know more than you're letting on. But this is no time to go into that. Just stick around where you can be reached, Professor. We'd appreciate that."

Luther was as surprised by Farner's news as Arnold had been.

"Herman Charnoff? What's it all mean, man? Why is he out to get you?"

Arnold thought it over.

"Well, I don't know that it's he who is out to get me. Just somebody with his car."

"But why? I mean, no offense, Arnold, but why the hell would anybody be after *you*? What have you got that anybody wants?"

Arnold drew himself up to full height in his chair.

"Well, as a matter of fact, there are some things about myself that I'm not at liberty to reveal."

Luther smiled at Arnold, then took a large bite of toast and chewed it thoughtfully.

"Things that you're not at liberty to reveal," he said with his mouth full. "My, my—how mysterious."

He swallowed the mouthful of toast.

"You mean like the fact that you're Alice Smythereene?"

Arnold choked on a swallow of coffee, spraying most of it onto the kitchen table, the residue running down the front of his pajama shirt. He coughed helplessly for several seconds.

"How the hell did you know about that?" he asked when the coughing fit had subsided.

"I didn't," Luther replied. "At least not till this moment. But it wasn't awfully hard to guess."

He grinned and tapped his temple with his index finger.

"Lodha, the detective. To begin with, it was obvious that Sherry Windsor didn't write those novels. I'm not even sure she can read them. And since Herman Charnoff is Alice Smythereene's agent, well, it sort of narrowed the field. And you've stayed in pretty close touch with him even though your last mystery story must have been five years ago. So it wasn't hard to put two and two together."

Luther waved his hand to take in their surroundings.

"Besides, you certainly have come up in the world in the last few years, haven't you? This apartment, a summer place, a new Mercedes. I know you publish poems, Arnold, but I don't think the *Kenyon Review* pays all that well. The income had to come from somewhere."

Arnold looked glum.

"That's what the police seem to be concerned about. I'm going to have to tell them about it. If you've guessed it other people may have as well. It's going to be hard to hide."

"Well," said Luther, "I have to admit I had something of an edge. You see, Sherry and I—well, we had a little affair a while back. A heat-of-the-summer romance. It only lasted a couple of weeks. She came on strong with me one night at one of Herman's parties. As a matter of fact, you ought to remember it. You took me there."

"Yes, I do. I suspected that something happened between you two, but I wasn't sure. It seemed especially confusing in light of my own, er, encounter with her so soon after."

"Encounter?"

Come Back, Alice Smythereene!

Arnold told of his brief fling with Sherry Windsor and of the wrenching effect on his domestic situation.

"Whew," said Luther when he had finished. "So that's why Elaine left. Too bad, man."

Arnold shrugged, then shook his head despairingly.

"Well," Luther continued, "I knew all along she was after something other than just my chocolate body. Beautiful though that may be. She was just too full of questions—about you, about me, what kind of things I wrote. Did I write prose or just poetry. Did I ever write under a pseudonym, did I know if you did. It was like getting it on with the CIA. Actually, I wasn't sorry when it ended. Though I didn't guess she'd find a replacement so soon."

The two sat in silence for several minutes until Arnold broke it by asking, "Luther, what do you suppose is behind it all?"

"I don't know, man. It sure is strange. Of course, there must be a hell of a lot of money in being Alice Smythereene. Who's your heir?"

"Oh, for crying out loud. Be serious."

"I am serious, man. *Cherchez le* profit motive, as they say. You must be worth a cool million."

"Luther, you're crazy. To begin with, Elaine is my heir, my one and only heir. I know she's mad at me, but I don't think she's reached the point of hiring a hit man. Besides, why would she have wanted to kill Pendleton? And anyway, I admit that Alice Smythereene has made me a bundle, but nothing like the amount you're suggesting."

Luther cocked an eyebrow.

"Come on, man. You're talking to Lodha Vishnu Dan. I wasn't reincarnated yesterday. If you haven't made over a million dollars out of those books, I'll eat a sacred cow."

"Luther, I swear to you. Not even half a million."

"Hey, man—you got a calculator?"

They sat at the kitchen table and worked it out. Arnold, who had no head for figures, could only guess at number of copies sold, prices and royalties. Luther punched the data into the calculator, copying the subtotals on a piece of paper as he went along. He rechecked the figures for several minutes before announcing his conclusion.

"Okay. A conservative estimate, my friend. *Conservative,* mind you. One million two hundred thousand dollars over the last four and a half years."

"Luther, I'm sure I didn't make more than a hundred thousand in any one of those years. And that's before taxes."

"Hey, taxes! Maybe it's spread out over a long time to avoid taxes. What kind of contract do you have?"

Arnold tried to remember.

"A standard contract. Herman drew it up."

"Standard contract? What do you mean, man? What's a standard contract?"

"A standard contract is a—a standard contract, that's all. I let Herman take care of it."

"Well, didn't you have a lawyer look it over?"

"No. I wanted to keep it all a secret. Besides, I trusted Herman."

Luther shot him a scornful look that made Arnold indignant.

"Herman and I have known each other for almost twenty years," he said defensively. "He's always been aboveboard with me."

Luther shook his head.

"That's fine, man. But there was never big bucks in it before. I don't want to tell you what to do, Arnold, but if I were you I'd take all the papers to a lawyer and let him look them over. You have them here? Or did Herman keep the only copies?"

Arnold resented the superior tone Luther was taking.

"Yes, I have the papers here. Everything from the initial contract for the first book. They're all in the file cabinet in my study. Wait here, I'll show them to you. Maybe you can give me the benefit of your fine legal mind."

Luther sighed. Arnold went to his study. There stood the battered metal filing cabinet in which were stored the precious documents of more than twenty years. Theatre programs, copies of income tax returns, book contracts, a Brooklyn Dodgers scorecard autographed by Sandy Koufax, all buried within the three drawers of that venerable piece of metal office furniture. It was a point of pride to Arnold that despite a reputation for vagueness he suffered among his friends, he could, in fact, put his finger on any document out of his past in a matter of seconds.

When a five-minute search failed to turn up the Alice Smythereene file, he felt a tug of panic. He emptied the drawers systematically, setting the contents in piles on the floor along the wall of the room. After fifteen minutes Luther joined him, and together they examined every piece of paper that had come out of the cabinet. Another hour was spent rummaging through desk and dresser drawers, closets and cupboards. All to no avail. Arnold had to face up to it. Every document, every piece of paper, every bit of evidence linking Arnold Simon to the million-dollar authoress Alice Smythereene had vanished from his possession.

Chapter 13

"It's Herman Charnoff, man. It's got to be. He's the key to the whole thing."

Luther punctuated his last sentence with a crunch, sending a cascade of crumbs, turkey shreds and Thousand Island dressing tumbling to the plate below. Arnold had never seen one of Milt's Number Two club sandwiches looking fatter, and he suspected Francine of lacing it with extra slices of turkey and swiss cheese. Luther ate with a gusto ill-befitting a minister of Vishnu, but any lapse of ascetic spirituality went unremarked by Francine. For Arnold's part, he had no appetite at all and picked cheerlessly at the shriveled piece of apple pie in front of him.

"It still leaves too many things unexplained," he countered. "Suppose you're right and Herman has been cheating me out of half my earnings. I don't believe it, mind you, but let's say so for the sake of argument. Why is he trying to *kill* me? And why kill Pendleton? It doesn't make sense. Not to mention Sherry Windsor's disappearance."

"More coffee, Lodha?"

Francine was back, standing at Luther's elbow.

"Francine, his name is Luther. Not Lodha. Luther." Arnold glowered at the girl. "Luther Washington."

"I like Lodha."

Luther beamed. He reached up and touched Francine's temples with his fingertips.

"Vishnu bless you," he told her.

"Om Vishnu Vishnaya," responded Francine.

"Oh, for God's sake," growled Arnold.

Francine stuck her tongue out at him before going off toward the kitchen.

"And another thing," Arnold resumed. "What about those racketeers the police talked about. How do they fit in? What connection would Herman have with them?"

"Well," replied Luther, "Herman Charnoff liked to gamble. We both know that. Half the time I tried to see him this summer he was at the track. Maybe he got hooked up with those guys that way. Maybe he owed them money."

"Oh my God! Maybe they killed him! Maybe he ran afoul of the mob and they did him in. Those things happen, don't they? That would explain why that thug Manuszak is riding around in Herman's car."

They stared at each other. Then Arnold shook his head.

"It won't do. Too many loose ends. How does Manuszak know so much about me? Why is Sherry missing? And what did Pendleton know? From the way he talked on the telephone I'm sure he knew that I'm Alice Smythereene."

Luther threw up his hands in a gesture of frustration.

"I don't know the answers, man. But it sure would be interesting to see the inside of old Herman's filing cabinet. The section under S, that is."

"I guess it would at that. I'd also like to have some evidence that I am Alice Smythereene next time your friend Farner wants to know how I made my money."

He smiled wryly at Luther.

"It's too bad your expertise was in car theft instead of

cat burglary, or else we could break in and steal the Smythereene file."

Luther sat bolt upright.

"Why not?"

"Why not what?"

"Break into Herman's office. I think I could find somebody to help us."

"Luther, are you crazy? I was just kidding. You can't . . ."

"We could do it tonight."

"Anyway, Herman doesn't have an office. He works out of his apartment."

"Yeah, I was just thinking of that. Central Park West between seventy-ninth and eightieth, right?"

"Seventy-eighth and seventy-ninth. But look, Luther . . ."

"I've been there a couple of times. That should make it easier."

He closed his eyes and furrowed his brow as if trying to visualize the layout. Arnold stared at him in horror.

"Luther, I'm not going to be a party to this."

"Eleventh floor, second door to the left coming off the elevator. Am I right?"

"You're out of your mind. You can't just break in. It's . . ."

Luther opened his eyes and glared at him.

"Shit, man. It's your *life* at stake here. Just trust me a little bit. Second door to the left off the elevator, right?"

"Third door to the left," said Arnold helplessly.

Arnold had the unpleasant sensation of being carried away on the tide of Luther's rising excitement. He badly needed a few minutes of calm to assess the situation, but Luther pressed on.

"Look, I've got to go find somebody. I'll meet you back here at four o'clock."

Luther looked at his watch, then corrected himself.

"Make that four-thirty. And on second thought, we'd

better not meet here. Let's make it your place at four-thirty. Got that?"

"Luther . . ."

Luther terminated the discussion by sliding out of the booth, colliding as he did so with Francine and causing her to drop a plate of blueberry pie.

"Forgive me, O flower of Vishnu. Arnold will pay for the pie."

He gripped Francine's waist and drew her to him, then lifted her half a foot off the ground until her face was level with his own. He kissed her noisily, set her down and glided toward the exit. Francine stared at his retreating figure until the street door closed behind him. Then, as if a spell had been broken, she reddened, and in a flustered voice demanded of Arnold, "What's going on?"

There was no time to reply. Luther was back, heading quickly to the table.

"Hey, man, I forgot. I'll need some money. How much you got?"

Arnold felt like a trapped animal.

"I don't know. About fifty dollars, I think."

"I'd better take it. There may be some immediate expenses. Oh—and it would help if you could get a couple hundred more in case we need it."

Luther held his hand out, and Arnold, with a sick feeling, took out his wallet and counted out sixty-one dollars. Luther put enough on the table to cover lunch and a fat tip. Francine watched the transaction with a puzzled look.

"Capital, sahib! I think we're in business," said Luther as he slipped the rest of the money into his pocket. "Don't forget the other two hundred. Four-thirty at your place."

Turning to Francine, he kissed the fingers of his right hand and placed them gently on her forehead.

"Later, beloved lotus. *Om Vishnu Vishnaya.*"

With that he was gone again. Arnold felt a knot in his stomach and wondered if he were going to be sick.

"Isn't he wonderful?" sighed Francine.

At four-thirty sharp they appeared at his apartment. Roger announced them over the house phone in a tone of obvious distaste.

"Your friend the, er, swami is here to see you, Mr. Simon. With another, er . . ." Roger groped for a word. "Individual."

"Send them up, Roger."

There was an audible sigh.

"Yes, sir."

Lower Fifth Ave. ain't what it used to be, Roger, old boy, thought Arnold as he replaced the receiver.

He was waiting at the open door when they got off the elevator. Luther was wearing a new turban, this one peach-colored with a large imitation emerald adorning the front. The lavender headpiece of the previous day now rested on the head of his companion.

"Arnold, this is Cyril. Cyril, this is Mr. Simon. He's your employer for the day."

"I never worked for nobody before," said Cyril. Then, turning to Arnold, he elaborated. "I always been self-employed."

Cyril stood scarcely over five feet and looked as if he weighed at most one hundred pounds. Luther's lavender turban sat just above his eyebrows. He wore a pair of faded, patched jeans several inches too short for him, revealing a stretch of sockless, pale shin above his black tennis shoes. Above the jeans was a torn blue T-shirt on which the words "Notre Dame National Champions 1977" were barely visible in faded gold letters. Against the chilly late September weather he wore an old brown overcoat, several sizes too large and stripped of buttons.

"Cyril was what you might call one of my classmates,"

explained Luther. "Upstate, I mean. He's fallen on hard times and could use some work."

"I never worked for nobody before," Cyril repeated. He looked around the apartment with an appraising eye that made Arnold extremely nervous.

"Uh, Cyril, could you excuse us for just a minute?"

Arnold pushed Luther into the kitchen.

"Are you crazy?" he asked in an agitated whisper. "What the hell are you planning to do?"

"Don't worry about it, man. Everything's gonna be cool."

"Cool? Cool? With that anorexic hobo in there? What the hell are you getting me involved in?"

Luther gave him a reproachful look.

"You know what, dad? You judge people too quickly. Old Cyril may not look like much right now, but believe me, man, he's an artist at his trade. A real craftsman."

"His trade?" sputtered Arnold. "What trade? Climbing into mailboxes to steal pension checks? Mugging midgets? Craftsman? Are you crazy?"

It suddenly occurred to Arnold that it might have been unwise to leave Cyril unattended in the foyer. He backed to the kitchen doorway and glanced out. Cyril had moved into the living room and was walking slowly along its periphery, studying the pictures on the walls. Arnold shuddered.

"Hey, man. Let me show you something." Luther stepped around Arnold and through the kitchen doorway.

"Hey, Cyril," he called out as he walked to the living room. Cyril turned and shuffled toward him with little mincing steps. The two stood huddled together, Luther speaking in a voice too low for Arnold to discern his words, until Cyril smiled at Arnold and raised two fingers to his forehead in salute. Then he moved birdlike to the entrance door and out of the apartment. Arnold stared after him in confusion.

"Arnold, lock the door," Luther instructed him. "Just like you do when you go out. Or to bed."

"I don't understand. Where did your friend go?"

"Just lock the door, man. Then let's go in the kitchen and have a beer."

"Luther, this is crazy. I . . ."

"Come on."

Luther pushed him gently toward the door, and Arnold bolted it. He secured both locks, the ordinary one furnished by the management and a heavy-duty deadbolt which he, an experienced New Yorker, had added on taking over the apartment. Then, once again under pressure from Luther, he allowed himself to be propelled toward the kitchen.

"You see, man? Everything's cool, like I told you. Now let's see what kind of brew you have on ice."

"Luther, I hope I didn't offend your friend. But I just worry that . . ."

"Think no more about it, dad."

Luther searched in the refrigerator and came up with two bottles of Molson's Golden Ale.

"The way I see it," he explained as he took the cap off the first bottle, "is that we have to get into Herman's file cabinet and see if we can find copies of your contracts with him. That way you have some evidence that you're Alice Smythereene. Then we try to find out if Herman's been skimming money off the top of your account. And also take a look at Sherry Windsor's file, if there is one, to see where she fits in with all of this."

He uncapped the second bottle and passed it to Arnold. Glancing at his wrist watch he said, "Let's take our beers in the living room. I think it's enough time."

"Time for what?" inquired Arnold.

Without answering, Luther left the kitchen. Arnold followed him out of the room, through the foyer and into the living room. Cyril was seated in an armchair fingering the porcelain figurine Arnold had splurged on in Munich the previous summer.

"This ain't real Meissen," said Cyril. "It's a fake. Made in England around 1900 is my guess. A lot of your what-you-call pastoral figurines were forged around then. You can spot them by the mark. It's too careful. I hope you didn't pay more than a couple hundred bucks for it."

Arnold gazed in shock at him.

"How did he get in here?" he asked Luther.

"That's his craft, man."

It was agreed, without dissent from Arnold, that he should take no part in the sortie against Herman's apartment. His role, as Luther saw it, was that of paymaster. The forty-odd dollars already supplied had, Luther explained, enabled Cyril to repossess the tools of his trade—a set of master keys and lockpicks—from his brother-in-law, who had been holding them as collateral against a small loan. An additional two hundred was now needed to furnish him with a decent set of clothes.

"What the hell does he need new clothes for?" a skeptical Arnold wanted to know. "Is it a semi-formal burglary or something?"

"For credibility, man," Luther explained. "When you operate in a high-price neighborhood like that you got to look the part. Show a little attitude. Three-piece suit, turban for exotic effect, maybe an attaché case. You have an attaché case?"

From all this planning Cyril remained aloof. As a specialist he was apparently not to be burdened with details concerning the financing of the operation. While Luther coaxed Arnold into this plunge into venture capitalism, Cyril moved sparrowlike around the living room, pausing from time to time to examine one of Elaine's carefully chosen appointments.

"Now this here what-you-call your nineteenth-century bronze, that's a good piece," he said softly, as if talking to himself. "Look at that signature, very crisp. And a real nice rubbed-on patina."

Arnold made a mental note to change the locks of the apartment at the earliest opportunity.

It was after midnight when they returned. Arnold had spent the evening watching television. The Mets, locked in the closing days of the season in a desperate battle for last place, had used six pitchers in a twelve-to-one pasting at the hands of St. Louis. After that the eleven o'clock news had highlighted an earthquake in southern California, a dioxin scare in Illinois, and an attempt to blow up the United States embassy in Islamabad. For relief Arnold turned to the late movie. The leader of a gang of jewel thieves, played by Michael Caine, sat languishing in prison while his sweetheart was being romanced by an international shipping tycoon. It was all too much for Arnold's frayed nerves, and he had just concluded that it would have been more restful to have accompanied Luther and Cyril on their caper when a voice behind him made him freeze in his chair.

"Them movie prison scenes ain't nothing like the real thing," said Cyril disapprovingly.

"Dear God!" Arnold exclaimed. He felt his heart pumping. "Couldn't you have just rung the bell?"

Cyril shrugged.

"Force of habit," he said.

Arnold had to admit that the change in Cyril was considerable. Dressed in gray flannel trousers, tweed jacket and cordovan shoes and carrying Arnold's attaché case, he had the air of a retired jockey with a winning investment portfolio. The turban had been abandoned.

"The Indian motif didn't fit Cyril, we decided," explained Luther. "Anyhow, it went off smooth as silk, and I brought back everything I could find relative to you and Alice."

Arnold cocked a questioning eye toward Cyril.

"Cyril just came back to say good-bye and borrow taxi fare home," said Luther.

"There wasn't much cash in that apartment," Cyril added apologetically. "Some other nice things, though. Good stamp collection. A 1930 Graf Zeppelin cover worth maybe four thousand on the open market."

Taxi fare turned out to equal the remaining fifty dollars Arnold had on hand, and it was with some difficulty that he restrained himself from asking whether Cyril lived in Ohio. The evening had so far cost him more than three hundred dollars, but he decided he would gladly write it off to have the affair done with. Besides, something helpful might come of Luther's wild scheme.

Cyril stayed for a farewell drink, a toast to his successful return to professional life, then departed into the night with his new attire, Arnold's attaché case and fifty dollars. As soon as he left Luther opened his own case and withdrew an assortment of envelopes and file folders.

"I didn't have time to go over things carefully, but as far as I could tell at a glance there is nothing in Herman's files connecting you and Alice Smythereene. It's like the K.G.B. was there, man, and decided to turn you into a non-person."

Luther's assessment was not entirely accurate. Arnold Simon existed as a person in the files of the Herman Charnoff agency until 1977 when the last of the A. A. Carruthers novels had been published. After that he made no appearance. As for Alice Smythereene, she turned out to be a corporation, with Herman Charnoff as president and Sherry Windsor as secretary. The last-named was also employed by Alice Smythereene, Inc., as a writer.

At least that is what Arnold and Luther were able to make of it. They sat in Arnold's kitchen eating bagels and lox and finishing the six-pack of Molson's as they tried to decipher the paragraphs of legal jargon and pages of figures.

"It's too much for me, man. But it sure don't look good," said Luther after they had been at it for over an hour.

"You can say that again."

Arnold was exhausted. He placed the documents back neatly into the attaché case and snapped it shut.

"I'm having lunch with Hadley Ottinger tomorrow. I think I'll take this along and ask him to look over the contents. It needs a lawyer to straighten it all out."

For tonight, he decided, he would keep it under his bed as he slept. His mind turned to burglaries and then to Cyril.

"By the way, Luther, there's one thing that puzzles me. What did Cyril get out of all this? I mean, he couldn't have done it all for a set of new clothes and a hundred bucks or so."

"Well," answered Luther slowly, choosing his words carefully, "he's been out of circulation for a long time, you know. I think it was important to him to work his way back into things."

Arnold was not convinced.

"Oh, come on. It's an awfully risky business for such a small reward."

The answer to his question occurred to him even before Luther spoke.

"Well, how can I put it, man? Do you ever read in the paper about some demolition job, maybe for the city or something, where the work is won by a very low bid in return for salvage rights to anything valuable that's torn down?"

"Salvage rights?"

"You might call it that."

Arnold wondered how fond Herman was of his stamp collection and how valuable it actually was. And he wondered if at that very moment there was, somewhere in the city, an unlisted dealer peering through a magnifying glass at a 1930 Graf Zeppelin cover. Whatever the hell that was.

Chapter 14

"Damn!" muttered Arnold into his newspaper the next morning at breakfast.

"What's the matter, dad?" asked Luther.

"Oh, nothing."

Arnold put down the paper. He looked morose.

"It's just that I have opera tickets for tonight. *Un Ballo in Maschera*. I just remembered."

He held up the *Times* so that Luther could see it and pointed to a picture of Luciano Pavarotti.

"Well, what's wrong with that?" asked Luther. "Do you good to take a night out, listen to somebody else's troubles."

"It's Elaine's favorite opera, and she's crazy about Pavarotti. I remember how excited she was last spring when she found out it was the opener of our subscription series."

He shook his head glumly.

"What a lot has changed since then."

"Why don't you call her up and see if she wants to go with you? It gives you an excuse to call."

"Do you think so?" Arnold looked skeptical. "I don't know. I called her last night, but Beverly said she was out. I think she just won't come to the phone. Anyway, it seems too frivolous to think of going to the opera with everything that's been happening. Do you want to use the tickets?"

"Little ol' frivolous me? No thanks, man. I still remember the last one. Look, why don't you just call Elaine and ask her to go. She's probably cooled down by now."

"Oh, I don't know. It just won't work."

Luther threw up his hands in exasperation.

"Oh hell, man. I'll do it for you. What's the number?"

"No, Luther, I don't think . . ."

"What's the number?"

Arnold told him the number. As Luther went to the phone he asked, "Who's the most famous child psychologist alive?"

"Huh? I don't know. Bruno Bettleheim, I suppose. Why?"

"Bettleheim. German?"

"Viennese, I think. Luther, what the hell are you up to?"

"Viennese?" Luther repeated as he dialed. "Like that fat little blond guy who played the waiter in *Casablanca*?"

Before Arnold could say 'S.Z. Sakall' Luther was speaking into the telephone.

"Ja, ah zo. Hallo dere. Dis is Herr Doctor Brrruno Beddleheim calling for Frau Doctor Zimon. Ja, Beddleheim, der pzychologist."

The accent was atrocious. As Arnold stared in disbelief Luther handed him the phone with a smile and a wink.

"They're getting her. It's all yours."

Arnold covered the mouthpiece with his hand.

"Luther, you're crazy. What am I supposed . . ."

Through the earpiece he heard Elaine's voice.

"Okay, this is Elaine Simon. Who are you and what do you want?"

"Hello."

Admittedly a weak response, but all Arnold could think of.

"I thought it was probably you," said Elaine. "As soon as I was told that there was some clown on the phone claiming to be Bruno Bettleheim with an accent like the fat little blond man who played the waiter in *Casablanca*."

Arnold looked at Luther in amazement.

"That fat little blond man," Elaine continued, "is what made me think of you."

"I don't think that's funny," replied Arnold.

"No, I agree. Not half so funny as calling up my clinic on a very busy morning, putting on a comic Viennese accent and pretending to be Bruno Bettleheim. Now *that's* what I call funny, Arnold. By God, you're the Mel Brooks of romance writers. All your little girl friends must be in stitches."

"Elaine, I didn't call up to start an argument. Why are you being so hostile?"

"Hey, man, that's no way to start," put in Luther from across the table. "You got to sweet-talk her."

"Hostile? You call this hostile?" Elaine was saying simultaneously. "Wait till you see me in court."

"And besides," said Arnold, his indignation mounting, "I don't have any little girl friends. You're being very unfair."

"I'm being unfair? What about that little scene I walked in on the other morning?"

"I could explain that if you would only give me a chance."

"Tell her you love her, man," prompted Luther. "You're handling this all wrong."

"Arnold, is someone there with you?"

"Tell her you love her," insisted Luther.

"Elaine, I love you."

It came out rather lame.

"Save it for your tootsies, Arnold," said Elaine, and hung up.

Arnold glumly handed the receiver to Luther to hang up.

"I told you it wouldn't work. She hung up."

"Aw shit, man. I got you your chance," said Luther. "You blew it."

Half an hour later, after Luther had gone out to attend to matters at the Temple of Vishnu, she called back.

"I'm sorry, Arnold. I shouldn't have lost my temper. We really have to make an effort to behave in a civilized manner, don't you think?"

"Elaine, if I could just see you, talk to you face-to-face. I'm sure I could explain."

He heard her sigh.

"I don't see how we can avoid seeing each other," she said, "if only to discuss a property settlement. I think we ought to be able to work it out intelligently, without bitterness."

"Property settlement? Who said anything about property settlement? I'm talking about seeing you. Tonight."

"Tonight is out of the question, Arnold."

"We have opera tickets. *Un Ballo in Maschera*, remember?"

"Oh. I forgot."

"The tickets are half yours, after all. It seems only right that we should share them. As a first step toward an intelligent property settlement."

"Very funny, Arnold. Well, I can't go tonight. I told Beverly . . ."

"Pavarotti's singing, remember? You were really looking forward to it."

"I know. So were you."

He could sense her wavering.

"We could each use one ticket. We don't have to talk to each other. Just listen to the music."

He began to sing into the phone in a broad, mock-operatic voice.

"La rivedrà nell'estasi, raggiante di pallor . . ."

He let the words roll lushly off his tongue.

"Oh, for heaven's sake, Arnold."

With scarcely a break in the melody line he switched into English, with the heavy accent of a phony Italian organ grinder.

> If-a you come-a with me to see *Un Ballo,*
> I'll be one great-a big happy-a fallo.

"Fallo?" said Elaine. "You're trying to make me laugh."

> I'll be so happy and-a content-a
> If you'll-a meet me at-a Lincoln Center.

She laughed a little.

> I'll-a be so good, I won't-a be naughty,
> We'll-a hear the great-a Pavaraughty.

"Oh, all right. Have mercy."

"You'll go?"

"I'll try. Anything to stop that wretched singing."

"How about dinner first?"

"Don't push me, Arnold. I'm not even sure I can go to the opera. I may have to fill in at one of Beverly's seminars tonight. I won't know until later this afternoon. How about my calling you later?"

"Sure. I'm having lunch with Hadley, but I'll be home from about three o'clock on."

"And Arnold . . ."

"Yes?"

"If it turns out I can go, don't read a lot into it. We're just sharing the opera tickets."

"Of course. Just two civilized people going to the opera."

But as he was shaving a few minutes later in preparation for his lunch with Hadley, he was struck by his good fortune. She had agreed to go out with him. They were going to have a date. It was like a new beginning.

"Hey-a buddy boy," he said aloud, waving his razor at the reflection in the bathroom mirror. "Everythings-a gonna be all-a right. She's-a gonna come back to you, ka-peesh?"

And a few minutes later, wiping his face with a towel, he added, "You one-a lucky sum-of-a-beech."

Arnold was fifteen minutes late arriving at La Fenice restaurant and found Hadley Ottinger already settled at a table.

"I took the liberty of ordering for both of us," the attorney informed him. "*Tortellini in brodo* followed by *pollo al peperone*. With a bottle of Orvieto classico, 1968."

"Fine, Had."

Arnold wished he were not so intimidated by his friend. He would have preferred spaghetti to tortellini, did not like pasta in broth, and favored beef over chicken. But Hadley brooked no contradiction in matters of food.

"Well," said the lawyer, chewing a breadstick, "how did your little declamation contest go the other night?"

"Declamation contest?"

"Poetry reading, creative writing orgy, whatever you call it. Did all your pubescent Ezra Pounds cover themselves with glory?"

Arnold was on the verge of telling Hadley about the attack on him en route to the All City Creative Writing contest and of his subsequent identification of the thug

Manuszak, when he remembered the lawyer's strict orders to avoid contact with the members of the NYPD special unit three. How was he to explain his riding there and back with Farner, not to mention his cooperation in going through the mug books without having informed his attorney? Better to let that story go for the time being.

"Oh, it was okay," he said. "But I have much bigger news than that."

He told Hadley of the burglary of Herman's apartment and of what the files had revealed. Hadley was aghast.

"Arnold, do you realize the penalty for suborning burglary? Are you out of your mind? I shouldn't even be sitting here and listening to this. Where are the files now?"

Arnold held up the attaché case which had been leaning against the leg of his chair. Hadley took it from him.

"I'd better take this with me and go through it at my office."

The waiter brought the *pollo al peperone* and they ate in silence for a few minutes. Arnold had to give Hadley credit for knowing his restaurant. The *pollo* was delicious, tender and glazed in a piquant wine sauce with just a hint of black pepper. He remarked on it to Hadley.

"What? Oh, yes. It's good, isn't it."

Ordinarily Arnold's praise would have been a cue to Hadley to discourse on the subtleties of northern Italian cooking and decry the peasant mentality of the general dining public in swallowing the tomato and garlic mess served up by most of New York's so-called Italian restaurants. But today he seemed distracted, troubled by Arnold's news.

"Herman Charnoff a crook? I can't believe that. We've known him too long."

He chewed meditatively on a piece of chicken.

"But you know," he went on, "your friend Washington has a point. Herman is a compulsive gambler. I've worried about that for some time now. I even tried to get him to go for professional help, see a psychiatrist, I mean. About a year ago. But Herman wouldn't hear of it. I guess like most people who need psychiatric help, he was afraid to admit he had a problem. And now that I think about it I wonder where he was getting all the money from."

He paused to wipe his mouth daintily with his napkin.

"And I mean big money, Arn. Herman wasn't making kid-sized bets. Either he had some hidden source of funds, or else he was piling up one hell of a debt. Maybe both. It scares me to think about it, you know? Those guys he was playing with don't fool around."

Hadley's concern was evident. When the waiter came he declined to order dessert. He sat staring thoughtfully at the cup of espresso coffee in front of him.

"Maybe we ought to go to the police," suggested Arnold.

"I think we'll have to do that eventually, but for the moment I'd rather hold off. To begin with, we have no real evidence that you are Alice Smythereene. But there's another, more important reason for not going to the police just yet."

He looked around uneasily.

"The fact is, Arn, that everything's not as it appears with the NYPD special unit three. Word is out that there's a leak. Someone is on the take. And until I can find out who we can trust there, I think we'd better keep away from those guys as much as possible."

"Farner said they'd want to talk to me soon."

"Well, there's no avoiding that, but make sure I'm with you. In the meantime I'm going to put a man of my own on the case, a private investigator who does an occasional job for me. We'll see what he can come up with in the next few days, by which time I ought to know whom we can trust at police headquarters."

The thought of taking action seemed to cheer him.

"You know, maybe we should have some dessert after all. I strongly recommend the *zucotto*. They make it with strega here, and so creamy you won't believe it."

By eight o'clock the crowd that had gathered in the Metropolitan Opera House lobby began to thin out, and within twenty minutes all that remained of it were a few small groups and a handful of individuals peering anxiously out into the rain-soaked plaza in search of some tardy companion. Arnold looked at his watch for the fifth time in as many minutes and decided it was hopeless. Elaine was not going to show up.

Not that he had come to Lincoln Center expecting much. When she had failed to call him back that afternoon he had tried to phone her, first at the clinic, then at Beverly's private number, both to no avail. At seven he had given up waiting and had taken a taxi to Lincoln Center in the thin hope of her showing up there. Puzzled and upset, he had prowled the plaza for more than thirty minutes until forced by the rain to take cover in the opera house lobby.

By eight-forty the lobby was virtually empty, and Arnold decided to give up. As he walked out into the chill late-September rain, he wondered what had gone wrong. It was unlike Elaine not to have called back. But then nothing in his life was as it should be lately. Perhaps her anger had flared up again, and she was punishing him by letting him dangle.

It had been a mistake, he realized, to wear a summer suit. He was by now drenched and chilled. Turning north on Columbus Avenue, he looked for a friendly bar where he could find shelter, a warming Scotch and perhaps even a companionable bartender.

* * *

It was one o'clock when he got home. As he entered the apartment he saw Luther step out of the bedroom and walk down the hall toward him.

"Uh, I'm not alone, man. Hope you don't mind."

He steered Arnold into the living room. A minute later Francine came in, smiling sheepishly.

"Hello, Arnold," she said.

Arnold giggled.

"Ah, Francine!" he exclaimed, placing one hand over his heart and extending the other toward her. "And I thought you loved only me. Fickle, fickle. Fickleness, thy name is woman."

He started to sing, but could not remember the words.

"*La donna è mobile*, tum tum ta tum-de-dum. Woman is fickle, fick, fick, fick, fickle."

"I'll make some coffee," said Francine, and headed toward the kitchen.

"Uh, how was the opera, man?" asked Luther.

"I know a poem about the fickleness of woman. Want to hear it?

> Go and catch a falling star,
> Get with child a mandrake root,
> Tell, uh . . .

He struggled to remember the words.

> Tell who blew up Francine's car,
> And gave Pendleton the boot . . .

"Or words to that effect," he concluded, grinning foolishly.

"Did you get to see Elaine?"

"Elaine? Fair but fickle."

"I take it she didn't show up."

Arnold dropped into the Queen Anne chair and closed his eyes.

"She didn't even call, old buddy."

Francine returned with a mug of instant coffee.

"Here, man, drink this," Luther urged, holding the coffee cup in front of him. "We have some important news about Alice Smythereene."

"Alice Smythereene? Who's that?"

"Oh, shit," said Luther.

"Oh, Alice Smythereene! I know her!"

Arnold began to recite.

> Oh Smythereene, my Smythereene!
> Historical romance's queen.
> Though other women let you down,
> She'll bring you fortune and renown.

"Is he always like this when he's drunk?" Francine asked Luther.

"You can usually tell how far gone he is by how bad the rhymes get."

> Book jackets showing goddesses
> With big boobs and torn bodices
> And lots of sex, not too obscene,
> Brought fame to Alice Smythereene.

"I'd say he's about half gone," said Luther as Arnold paused to think of another couplet.

> But where's the money? Ask the goniff
> Known to the world as Herman Choniff.

He grinned at Luther.

"*Goniff* is the Yiddish word for thief. Choniff the goniff. Of course, his name's not really Choniff, but what the hell—poetic license."

Luther groaned.

"Better make some more coffee," he told Francine.

It was not until Arnold was on his third cup of coffee that Luther told him of his most recent discovery.

"The fact is, man—Sherry Windsor is not Sherry Windsor. Or at least she wasn't until two years ago, when she had her name changed."

"Name changed?"

Arnold squinted at Luther in an effort to understand.

"You see, the Alice Smythereene file I, er, liberated from Herman's apartment contained a certain amount of information about Sherry. In particular, her social security number."

"Social security number?"

"Then this afternoon Francine happened to mention that her brother-in-law works for social security."

"Brother-in-law?"

"My sister's husband," explained Francine.

"So she agreed to call and ask him to run a check on Sherry's number."

"He's really not supposed to do it," said Francine. "He could get in trouble."

"Well, nobody's going to rat on him," Luther told her.

"Rat?"

Arnold wished Luther would make things clearer and not drag them out. He had an awful headache and wanted to go to bed.

"Anyway, it turns out that Sherry Windsor's social security number wasn't issued to anyone named Sherry Windsor. It was issued to a woman named Manuszak. Marilyn Manuszak. Wife of Leonard. What do you make of that?"

Chapter 15

After Luther and Francine had departed, Arnold dozed fitfully in his armchair. A queasy stomach and a throbbing head prevented him from sleeping restfully. In a dream he saw Elaine and himself standing on the great stage of the Metropolitan Opera, arms around each other as their voices swelled in the love duet from *Un Ballo in Maschera*, while looking on from the wings was big, ugly Lenny Manuszak. At his side, her red mouth twisted in a mocking grin, stood Sherry.

He came wide awake and sat upright in the chair, eyes wide open. The thought of Elaine bobbed to the surface of his consciousness, and a vague sense of unease now congealed into a single question. Had something bad happened to her? The question had not presented itself to his conscious mind until then, and he cursed the excess of self-pity that had kept him from considering the possibility of harm coming to Elaine.

He closed his aching eyes for several seconds, then opened them to peer at his wrist watch. It was two-thirty. Never mind the hour, he thought, to hell with the time. He had to call and make sure Elaine was safe at home.

He rose stiffly from the armchair and made his way haltingly to the bedroom. Sitting on the edge of the bed he tried to recall Beverly's number. He stared in concentration at the dial and slowly dialed what he hoped was the right one. After the twelfth ring he lost heart and was on the verge of hanging up when the receiver was lifted at the other end.

"Hello?" Beverly's voice, hoarse with sleep but recognizable.

"Beverly, this is Arnold. I'm sorry to wake you, but I have to talk to Elaine. Is she there?"

"Arnold?" She sounded confused.

"Yes. I know it's awfully late, but . . ."

"You're all right, then? Thank goodness."

"Of course I'm all right. What are you talking about? Is Elaine there?"

"Isn't she with you?" Beverly now sounded fully awake. "Aren't you at the hospital? I just assumed she was spending the night there."

"What hospital? Beverly, what the hell are you talking about?"

The doorbell was ringing. Arnold was seized by a feeling of panic.

"I'm sorry, Beverly. I missed what you just said."

"Well—she got a phone call from the police about three o'clock this afternoon saying you were the victim of a hit-and-run driver and were in serious condition. She left immediately to go to the hospital. The last I saw of her was as she was getting into a cab. Dear God, Arnold—haven't you seen her?"

Now it was Beverly's turn to be gripped by panic.

"Arnold, what's going on? Wasn't it true? Wasn't it the police who called?"

The ringing of the doorbell had become incessant. Now it was joined by the house telephone.

"Beverly, can you hang on a minute? Somebody's at the door."

He placed the receiver on the night table and moved

quickly to the front door. There stood Hadley Ottinger, bright and wide-awake in a black leather jacket and a pair of jeans.

"Arn, throw on a coat and come with me. There's no time to waste, we've got to get moving. The game's afoot."

As Arnold stared uncomprehendingly at Hadley, the house telephone resumed its insistent buzz.

"Uh—come on in. I've got someone on the phone."

He moved from the door to the house phone.

"Hello?"

"Mr. Simon, your attorney friend Mr. Ottinger is here to see you."

Something had to be done about building security, thought Arnold.

"Yes, I know, Roger. He's here with me now."

"Odd hour to call, wouldn't you say, sir?"

"I'm busy right now, Roger. I don't have time to discuss the visiting habits of my friends."

He hung up abruptly and ran toward the bedroom.

"Hello, Bev. Are you still there?"

"Arnold, what's going on?"

"What hospital did Elaine go to?"

There was a moment's silence.

"Dear Lord, I don't know. She never said, and I didn't think to ask. Everything happened so quickly."

"Who was it that called? Did you get his name?"

"Yes. I answered the phone myself. Let's see, it was Barnum or Farnum, something like that. Maybe Farley."

Arnold felt dizzy. He propped himself on the night table.

"Was it Farner?"

"It could have been. Yes, I think it was. Why? What's going on? Is Elaine all right?"

Arnold sat down on the bed.

"I don't know, Beverly. I don't know what's going on."

From the living room came the voice of Hadley Ottinger, loud and urgent.

"Arnold, we've got to get moving."

"Beverly, I've got to go. Somebody is here waiting for me. I'll call you back as soon as I know something."

"But, Arnold . . ."

He hung up before Beverly could complete her sentence. As he started to rise he was overcome with lightheadedness, so he sat on the edge of the bed leaning forward with his head between his knees and breathed deeply. From the doorway Hadley spoke to him, talking in a lower but still excited tone.

"Arn, you have to pull yourself together. We've got things to do. I just heard from Herman, about an hour ago."

Arnold straightened up slowly until he was facing Hadley. He gazed stupidly at him for a few moments before answering.

"Hadley, something's happened to Elaine."

"I know. She's been kidnapped. That's one of the things I learned from Herman. It was engineered by that black cop, Farner. I told you that one of those special unit guys was on the take. Well, there you have it."

Arnold stared in disbelief.

"Don't panic, Arn. It'll be okay. Elaine won't come to any harm, as long as we do what we're supposed to. At least that's what Herman assured me."

"What do we have to do? Where are we going?"

"I'll tell you the whole story in the car. We've got a five-hour drive ahead of us to get to Herman. He's been hiding out in the country for the last two weeks."

"But where? Where are we going?"

"To your summer place up in Vermont."

The lighted dial on the speedometer of Hadley's Porsche registered eighty miles per hour as they sped north along the New York State Thruway. Arnold stared at it as he listened to Hadley tell of his recent conversation with Herman Charnoff.

"He's been holed up at your summer house for about two weeks, hiding out from the mob. He says you gave him a key and permission to use the place."

"Yes, that's right."

Arnold now remembered that Herman had asked to use the Simons' summer retreat for a weekend getaway a few weeks earlier.

"It's pretty isolated up there this time of year. But, Hadley, who exactly is the mob?"

"Well, I'm not sure. Those people the police mentioned to you, I guess. Herman's been mixed up with some pretty bad company for a few years now. All because of his compulsive gambling. He got pretty heavily into debt with them, and they've been using him to help them push drugs. Around the publishing world, I mean."

"Herman a drug pusher?"

Arnold sounded incredulous.

"Well, I think the actual pusher was Pendleton. They pressured Herman into signing him on as a writer and acting as front man for him. I suspect his books were ghosted."

Hadley's tone became more confidential.

"Actually, I purchased a bit of coke myself through Pendleton."

Arnold watched the speedometer move up to eighty-five.

"In the past few months," Hadley continued, "there's been some sort of feud going on. Herman wasn't very clear about the details, but I got the impression he was caught in the middle of it. Pendleton, too. With rather disastrous consequences, as you know."

Arnold shuddered.

"Hadley, what's happened to Elaine? Is she all right?"

"I'm coming to that. Arnie, I hate to tell you this, but your friend Washington was right. Herman has been stealing from you. About half a million dollars over the last five years. Herman was very contrite about it. Said he never meant for it to go that far. Just saw it as a way to pay off some of his debts to the mob and keep them off his back, but it got out of hand. What's more to the point is that just before leaving for Vermont he had closed a deal with ABC television for a mini-series based on one of your novels. On one of Alice Smythereene's novels, that is."

"Yes. *Mallory's Mistress*. I remember reading about it in the newspaper and wondering what it was all about. Herman never said anything to me about it. But what's that got to do with Elaine?"

"Arn, give me a chance to explain it the way Herman told it to me. To begin with, that mini-series will bring you—or the Alice Smythereene company, whoever that is—two million dollars. And there are plans to expand it to a regular series if it catches on. The whole deal would be worth four or five million. Right now Herman is holding a cashier's check for a quarter million. He's kept himself alive for the last few months by waving this deal in front of his mafia buddies, selling himself as the goose who's about to lay the golden egg, and playing on their greed for future millions."

"But what about me? What did they gain by coming after me? If there was any golden egg, I was the goose who was going to lay it."

"It seems they were aware of that. You were sort of Herman's collateral, Arn. There was no profit for anyone in seeing you dead. But in the last few weeks the boys have been getting impatient, beginning to doubt Herman's good faith. So they decided to put a little pressure on him. According to Herman, those so-called attempts on your life weren't intended to kill you. Only to scare him."

"And Elaine?"

"More or less the same thing. You know, Herman's been playing a pretty dangerous game, trying to stave off his mob friends with one hand and complete the TV deal with the other, all the while keeping the quarter-million down payment on the series for himself. The trouble is that he's been fooling around with some mean characters, and they're not about to let him get away with it. They've snatched Elaine and they're holding her for security until they get some money from Herman. He finally agreed to give them the quarter million as a gesture of good faith, in which case they've agreed to let Elaine go unharmed. Which is why we're now on our way to Vermont. We're acting as messengers. We pick up the check from Herman, bring it back to New York, convert it to cash and buy your wife back from the gangsters who are holding her."

They rode in silence while Arnold absorbed the impact of Hadley's information. Finally he asked, "Where does Sherry Windsor fit into all this?"

"I'm not sure. All I know is that Herman discovered her through Pendleton, whose mistress she was. I assume it was pressure from Pendleton or his bosses that got her on the payroll. But just what her function was and what's happened to her are mysteries to me."

They were still hours from their destination, and Arnold felt immensely tired. He leaned back in the seat and closed his eyes.

"It's probably a good idea for you to get some sleep," said Hadley, observing him out of the corner of his eye.

There remained a number of unanswered questions, loose ends too tangled to sort out. Hadley's story required further thought, but Arnold was too tired to give it his attention. One question bothered him, however, and he asked it before falling asleep.

"Had, if Herman has been hiding out for the last few weeks, and if they don't know where he is, then how has he communicated with them?"

There was a long silence during which Hadley stared straight ahead at the road. After a while he cleared his throat and spoke in a low voice.

"Through me. I'm sorry, Arn, but I couldn't tell you before. Herman made me swear. He's been desperate. I've been involved in this business since last week, trying to negotiate for him and still look out for your best interests. And keep everybody, including myself, from getting hurt. It's been a hell of a strain."

By the time Arnold awoke they had left the Thruway. The sky was turning light, a cold, steel gray that promised rain. The morning chill made Arnold shiver, and he huddled in the corner of his seat.

"I'll turn up the heat," said Hadley. "You'll feel warmer in a minute. We can stop for coffee in a little while."

Arnold realized he was wearing the same summer suit in which he had stood in the rain at Lincoln Center so many hours ago waiting for Elaine. He wondered where she was, whether she was safe and comfortable, whether she was frightened. He longed to see her.

He looked out the window and tried to determine where they were. From what he could make out they were already in Vermont, heading north on U.S. 7 toward Bennington. He reckoned it must be close to seven o'clock. As Hadley had promised, the car was now warm to the point of coziness. Arnold yawned. He rested his head on the window, and, despite the coldness of the pane, managed to fall back to sleep.

Hadley woke him as they approached Wilmington.

"You're going to have to guide me from here, buddy. Let's stop in Wilmington and get some breakfast."

The village was just awakening as they drove down its main street. In front of the variety store a young woman was industriously sweeping the sidewalk, while the grocer next door fussed over a display of produce. Across the street a tiny lady in a pink-and-white apron was unlocking the door of the Village Waffle Shoppe whose window proclaimed "Breakfast Special: Juice, Coffee, Two Eggs Any Style, $1.99."

"Come on," said Hadley as he drew the car alongside the curb and switched off the engine. "Let's get something to eat before we face Herman. Anyway, I have to call my office. I forgot to cancel one of my appointments for today."

The street was almost empty, the village in a hiatus between tourist seasons—too late for summer visitors, too early for skiers.

"Mornin', gents. What'll it be?" asked the lady in the pink-and-white apron as they entered the waffle house. "Batter is fresh and the iron's hot."

"We'll have orange juice, coffee and blueberry waffles," replied Hadley before Arnold could say anything. "And point me toward the phone, please."

Arnold sat at the counter and drank a cup of coffee while Hadley made his call. From where he sat he could see through the shop window to the stores across the street. He watched two elderly ladies turn into the small supermarket. They were almost knocked down by a large man as he exited hurriedly. Arnold froze at the sight.

"Oh my God!" he whispered. His hand trembled as he set his cup down. He jumped off the stool and ran to the door of the restaurant, then opened it and peered down the street in time to see the big man getting into a large yellow Buick. Arnold turned back into the restaurant just as Hadley took a seat at the counter.

"Had! It's Manuszak! I've seen him. He's here!"

Hadley jumped off his stool and ran to the door which Arnold held open. Together they stepped outside and watched Herman Charnoff's Buick turn a corner and head north toward Route 100.

"That's the direction to my place!" said Arnold excitedly.

"We'd better follow him," said Hadley.

"Waffles are ready, gents," called the tiny lady from behind the counter.

They ran to Hadley's car. As they were getting in, the lady from the waffle house came out to the street and shouted, "Hey, there! What am I supposed to do with these waffles?"

Ignoring her, Hadley gunned the car forward.

"Damned out-of-staters," she called after them.

Five miles north on Route 100 they caught sight of the Buick. Hadley, who had been doing eighty, eased his foot off the accelerator.

"I don't want to get too close—just keep him in sight."

"The turn-off to our place is just up ahead," Arnold told him. "Be ready to make a left in case that's where he's going."

The words struck him as pointless. There could scarcely be another place in the state of Vermont where Manuszak was going. Sure enough, in less than two minutes the big Buick turned off the highway and onto the gravel road that was the last leg of the journey. Hadley pulled the car over to the side of Route 100 and shut off the engine.

"Since it's obvious where he's going, there's no point in following him," he explained. "If we get too close behind him on that road it will be obvious that we're tailing him. And there goes any advantage of surprise we might have."

"Maybe we should go back and call the police," suggested Arnold.

"Well, I'm a little afraid of getting them involved and maybe upsetting Herman's plan. God knows what harm could come if we get those mobsters upset. We'd better take a look-see up at your cabin first. If we're quiet about it, Manuszak won't even see us. Then if it looks like trouble we can scoot back to town and call the police."

"That could be awfully dangerous. Why don't we . . ."

They were moving before Arnold could finish.

"I think we've given him enough of a start," said Hadley as he turned the car onto the gravel road.

They drove uphill to a point where a dirt road branched off to the right, descending into a forest of evergreens.

"Follow the dirt road," said Arnold. "We're about a mile and a half from the cabin now. Maybe we ought to park a little distance away so he doesn't hear us coming. Maybe a quarter mile or so. I'll tell you where."

Hadley drove slowly until Arnold told him to stop. Then they left the car and went on foot. After five minutes they could see the cabin. The Buick was parked in a clearing at its side. There was no other car in sight.

"Let's get closer and see what's up," whispered Hadley.

They left the road and walked as quietly as they could through the strand of trees flanking its side. By moving deeper into the woods they were able to skirt the house and come up on its rear without leaving the cover of the trees. Between the woods and the house was a clearing of some fifty feet. Arnold stood behind a tree at the edge of the clearing, gathering his nerve and wondering what to do next. He was amazed at his boldness in having come this far. Well, he thought—too late to be nervous now.

He looked at Hadley, who motioned him to move toward the house. Arnold took a deep breath, dropped to a crouch, and, keeping below the line of sight from the cabin windows, ran across the clearing and dropped to his knees alongside the house. He pressed close to the wall and crawled along it until he was underneath a window. Then raising himself slowly, he peered inside.

Elaine sat facing him, tied to a chair at the opposite end of the room. Next to her stood the hulking Manuszak, and facing them both, seated on a couch and holding a gun, was the woman variously known as Marilyn Manuszak, Sherry Windsor and Alice Smythereene.

"I think we'd better go inside now."

Hadley's voice came full strength from behind him. Arnold was stunned by his friend's stupidity in speaking so loudly, and with finger on lips, still crouching, he turned to face him. He was surprised to see that Hadley was holding a gun. He was even more surprised to see that it was pointed directly at his chest.

"Sorry, Arn," said Hadley. "End of the road."

Chapter 16

Arnold had to admit it was a cozy scene. Early morning in Vermont. A fire burning in the hearth, driving the late September chill from the room. The smell of fresh-brewed coffee mixing deliciously with the odor of burning pine cones. And a glimpse through the window of steel gray sky and light, steady rain adding a pleasant twinge of melancholy to the mood.

A scene to warm the heart. Marred only by the sight of Elaine tied to the chair next to his and by the bite of the rope as Manuszak tightened it around his legs.

Elaine looked pale and tired and frightened.

"Elaine . . ." He found it hard to speak. His throat felt constricted.

"Oh, Arnie. I'm sorry. I feel so stupid. I just went to pieces when I heard you'd been hit by a car. Then when I found out it wasn't true . . ."

She bit her lip as tears appeared in her eyes. Arnold fought his own impulse to cry.

"Elaine . . ." He wanted to tell her it was his fault, not hers. He wanted to tell her that somehow they would get out of it. He wanted to tell her he loved her. But the words would not come. He was unable to speak.

"It's okay, Arnie. You don't have to say anything. I understand."

She took a deep breath and held it for a moment, fighting to regain her composure. Then she smiled at him, a little rueful half-smile, as tears ran down her cheeks.

"It's a fine mess you've gotten us into, Ollie," she said softly in her Stan Laurel voice.

Arnold tried to smile back. It was important that they not go to pieces.

"Did they hurt you?" he asked.

She shook her head. "How about you? Are you all right?"

"I'm okay." This time he succeeded in smiling. "Though on the whole I'd rather be at *Un Ballo in Maschera*."

She smiled back. "Well, at least you succeeded in getting us back together."

Manuszak had almost finished tying Arnold to his chair. He pulled hard on the rope.

"Ouch! That really hurts. Must you pull it so tight?"

Manuszak did not answer.

"It's no use, Arnie," Elaine told him. "I don't think he speaks English. Try Cro-Magnon."

Watching the scene from his place on the sofa, Hadley grinned appreciatively. Manuszak responded by pulling tighter on the rope cutting into Arnold's legs.

"God damn it!" Arnold swore. "You're cutting off my circulation. Hadley, can't you tell him to loosen up a bit? I'm not going anywhere."

"He don't tell me nothing," said Manuszak. They were the first words Arnold had ever heard him speak. The voice was surprisingly high-pitched, as if a moose had opened his jaws wide and emitted the sound of a hyena. The effect was chilling.

Arnold looked enviously at Hadley sitting comfortably on the couch, drinking hot coffee and eating a buttered roll.

"How much of what you told me on the way up here was true?" he asked.

"About half." Then, after a short pause. "On second thought, maybe a third."

The attorney smiled brightly. At that moment Arnold would have given anything in the world for a chance to punch him.

"What about Herman?" he asked. "Where is he?"

Hadley waved a hand in the direction of the woods in back of the house.

"Out there. We buried him a week ago yesterday."

"Yeah," said Sherry, entering from the kitchen. "One of these days we'll have to think about putting up a tombstone."

She gave a brief husky laugh and smiled in Arnold's direction. The perfect whiteness of her teeth was accented by her deep tan. She wore a pair of snug jeans and a plain white T-shirt with no bra underneath, so that the large nipples of her heavy breasts were clearly outlined. Arnold noticed the hungry look with which Hadley watched her cross the room, and he could sense Manuszak's tension.

"Enter the Empress Messalina in tight T-shirt," said Elaine dryly. "All males begin panting in unison."

Arnold realized he was breathing heavily.

Ignoring Elaine's remark, Sherry poured a mug of coffee and carried it to Manuszak.

"Here, Lenny sweetheart. Drink this. Then you better get started for the city."

"Why do I have to be the one to go?" Manuszak asked sulkily. "Why can't he go?"

He pointed a bear paw at Hadley.

"Oh, for crying out loud," said Ottinger in a peeved tone. "We've been through this a dozen times."

"Aw come on, honey," said Sherry sweetly to the pouting hulk. "You know you're the only one who can do the job. We can't leave it to Hadley now, can we? He can't do what you can."

She stood so close that her chest was touching him. One of her hands caressed his cheek; the other rested on his upper forearm.

"Come on outside for a minute. I want to talk to you where they can't hear."

She walked to the door and beckoned him to follow, her mouth curled in a fetching pout. Lenny obeyed her like a trained bear. As they left the cabin together Arnold saw her slip an arm about his waist.

"Lovely little menagerie you have here, Had," said Elaine when the door had closed behind them.

Hadley shrugged.

"She can get him to do anything she wants. It's useful."

Hadley's air of unconcerned pragmatism was spoiled by his look of consternation. He stared balefully at the closed front door.

"Why did you kill Herman, Had?" Arnold asked him. "And why are you keeping us here like this? What's going on?"

The lawyer did not answer at first, seemingly reluctant to transfer his concentration away from the closed door and his thoughts of what might be taking place on the other side. After a minute, however, he regained control of himself.

"Well, let's see. Where should I begin? Part of what I told you was true. Herman did get up to his nostrils in gambling debts, and the mob did use him as a conduit for passing drugs to customers in literary circles. With Pendleton set up as one of Herman's authors so he could run the operation. And, oh yes, Arn, he was cheating you. He must have done you out of a cool half million. Not that that's why we, er, eliminated him."

He smiled at Arnold.

"You see, Arn, Herman never really wanted to be a bad guy. In fact he was very remorseful about what he was doing to you. It's just that he got in over his head and didn't know what to do. Until one day he saw a way out. One of the TV networks expressed an interest in making a four-part mini-series out of an Alice Smythereene blockbuster, and Herman was smart enough to parlay it into a two-million-dollar deal with the hope of even more from a regular series follow-up. He figured that with his share of the proceeds he could buy his way out of the rackets and also pay back what he owed you. Or at least pay back enough to keep you from prosecuting him while he figured out some way to make good on the rest. The poor chump actually planned to confess everything to you, Arn—throw himself on your mercy. But not until he could make a sizable restitution. Poor Herman. He wanted everybody to like him."

Hadley shook his head sadly.

"There was just one fly in the ointment. Pendleton. He kept nosing into Herman's affairs, using Sherry as a spy. She and he had been rather, uh, close at one time."

"Was that while she was married to Manuszak?" asked Arnold.

Hadley looked surprised.

"So you found out about that, did you? Well, yes. Pendleton sort of stole her from Lenny, and Lenny never forgave him for it. That's what made it so easy to get Lenny to handle him when the time came. But I'm getting ahead of the story."

From outside came the sound of a car starting. Hadley stopped speaking and stared at the front door. After a few moments Sherry entered the house.

"Boy, it's chilly out there."

"You were out there long enough," said Hadley sullenly. "What the hell were you doing all that time?"

"Just sitting in the car. I had to get him in an agreeable mood, didn't I? He doesn't like you very much, you know."

She headed toward the bedroom.

"I'm going to put on a sweater."

"After that, how about making something to eat? I'm starving. And we'd better feed these two."

Hadley nodded toward Arnold and Elaine. Sherry looked as if she were about to object, then shrugged her shoulders.

"Yeah, okay," she said as she went into the bedroom.

"Where was I?" Hadley resumed. "Oh, yes. Pendleton. Well, he had an idea that Herman was fudging the Alice Smythereene account, and he knew there was a big deal in the works, but the one thing he didn't know was the true identity of Alice Smythereene. With that information he figured he could really put the squeeze on Herman. Blackmail, I mean. Of course, he knew that Sherry wasn't the real Alice, and it was easy to narrow the field down to just a few. So he sent Sherry out on a couple of Mata Hari expeditions to see what she could find out. She tried your friend Luther first. Dumb choice in my opinion, but I guess she had to start somewhere. You were next, and—bingo! It didn't take much, she told me. A little sweet talk, a little interest, one toss in the sack and you were ready to spill all. Cripes, Arn, you were a pushover! You poor simp. You could have been banging her for a month. Oh, sorry, Elaine."

Elaine looked at Hadley intently.

"Just once, Hadley?" she asked. "Wasn't there a second time?"

"Second time?" echoed Sherry, coming out of the bedroom. "The second time was a zero, sweetheart. Your husband couldn't have done anything even if he wanted to. I doped up his drink. The idea was to put him out for a while so I could look through his papers."

She stood next to Arnold and ran her hand through his hair.

"Not that I think he could have done much anyway. Not after the first time. I never saw anybody so hung up with guilt over a lay. You got one hell of a tame animal, lady."

She crossed the room and exited into the kitchen. Arnold looked at Elaine. There were tears in her eyes.

"Elaine, I'm sorry," he told her. "Really I am. When we get out of this I'm going to make it up to you."

"No, Arnie. It was my fault. I was too unyielding. I'm sorry, Arnie. I love you."

Her voice faltered. Hadley beamed at them.

"Gosh, it's really nice to see two people who really care about each other. It reaffirms your faith in human nature."

Arnold glared at him.

"Anyway," he continued, "to get back to what I was saying. When Pendleton found out that you were Alice Smythereene he sent Sherry to Herman with a proposition. A fifty-fifty split on the TV profits or else he would spill the beans to you. Poor Herm. He was on the verge of a nervous breakdown. Negotiations with the network were delicate, he was being pressed by his mobster friends to pay up, and now he was threatened with exposure as a thief. Everything was coming down on his head at once. He figured that if only he could hold Sherry off for four or five days—poor jerk, he didn't realize Pendleton was behind it, he thought she was acting on her own—if he could only keep her quiet for a while, he'd close the deal and everything could be set right."

Hadley smiled.

"That's where I come in," he resumed. "I ran into

him one day just when he was at his lowest point, inches away from a collapse. He just let go and told me the whole story. Asked me for advice. Well, together we hatched a plan. Kidnap Sherry, keep her out of town for a few days, enough time for Herman to work everything out. No harm, you understand. Just keep her incommunicado. That's when he asked you for the use of this place. And I took a few days off from work to stay up here and guard her. It seemed the least I could do for a friend.

"What Herman didn't count on—what I didn't count on myself—was what would happen when Sherry and I were alone together up here. Arn, I can't describe what it was like. There was the most gorgeous full moon you ever saw. The evenings were still, not a soul around. The nights were beautiful. She was beautiful. By the third day I was in love. Head over heels. Really in love for the first time in my life."

Arnold stared at him in disbelief.

"Hadley, do you know how many times you've said that to me? Are you crazy? What have you gotten yourself into?"

"Give me some credit. I know what I'm doing. Sherry and I are crazy about each other. She's magnificent. A bit unpolished, perhaps, but I can fix that."

"What a touching little triangle, Hadley," said Elaine. "Just you and her and the ape man."

"Yes," responded Hadley. "Well, his time is coming soon."

"I still don't understand why you killed Herman," said Arnold.

"Well, during the four days we spent together up here—and, Arn, they were the most wonderful four days of my life—it occurred to us that with the exception of a few people the whole world thinks Sherry Windsor is Alice Smythereene. So if we just eliminated those few people she could go on being Alice Smythereene. The network money would be ours. Millions. More money than you can imagine. Not to mention money from future books. Arn, we're sitting on a gold mine."

Hadley's eyes shone with a fervor almost religious in its intensity.

"Hadley, you're mad," whispered Arnold.

Hadley shrugged.

"Men have done stranger things for less. What did we have to do, after all? Get rid of Herman—that was easy. I got him to come up here and, well, it was easy. Then there was Pendleton. He knew too much. So we sent Lenny to take care of him. As I told you, Lenny already had it in for him."

"And what about you, Had? Doesn't he have it in for you? You're doing the same thing to him that Pendleton did."

"Yes, but the poor chump doesn't know it. He thinks I'm just in it for the money, and he's perfectly willing to split that with me as long as he gets his own true love back."

Hadley smiled.

"You see, Sherry and I decided it was best to keep Lenny in the dark about our future plans. Right now he's gone to do a little job for us. Then when he comes back he'll take care of you two. Sorry, Arn, but that's the way it is. Sorry, Elaine."

"Oh, don't mention it, Hadley," she replied. "What's a life between friends."

"Well, anyway, after he finishes that for us, then . . ."

He made the motion of cocking a gun with his thumb and index finger.

"Good-bye, Lenny," he said.

Sherry, who had returned from the kitchen with a platter of sandwiches and a large bag of potato chips, frowned at Hadley's last words.

"Is that lunch?" Hadley asked incredulously, eyeing the bag of potato chips with displeasure.

"I'm not a friggin' cook," answered Sherry.

Displeasure or not, Hadley ate hungrily. When he had finished he untied the arms of his captives while Sherry stood watch with a gun.

"God, I'm exhausted," he announced as Arnold and Elaine ate their sandwiches. "I'm going to catch a couple of hours' sleep. We've got a long wait, kids. It'll take Lenny about five hours to get to the city, an hour or so to take care of his errand and another five to get back. That should bring it to eight o'clock tonight. Maybe a little later."

After they had eaten he retied them. Then he looked at Sherry and jerked his head in the direction of the bedroom.

"Say, my darling. Why don't you keep me company for a while?"

"Get out of here," she replied. "You're out of your mind. Who's gonna watch them?"

"They're not going anywhere. Lenny did a good job. Those ropes are very secure. Come on, just for a little while. Arnie and Elaine would probably like to be alone for a bit."

He walked over to her, put his arms around her and began nuzzling her neck. Backing toward the bedroom, he dragged her after him. She protested, but not wholeheartedly.

"Hadley, are you nuts? Let me go. This is embarrassing."

Hadley kissed her ear. She started to giggle. At the bedroom door he stopped and winked in Arnold's direction.

"Ol' Rick Rheingold never had it so good, eh, Arn?"

A troubling thought had been nagging at Arnold.

"Hadley," he asked, "what business is Lenny taking care of for you in the city?"

Hadley looked sheepish.

"Well, Arn, don't think too badly of me. When we started this we thought we'd only have you and Elaine and Herman to contend with. And Pendleton, of course. But now your friend Luther Washington is in on the act. So I made arrangements with him on the phone this morning. That was Luther I called from the waffle shop in Wilmington. I made arrangements to meet him at two o'clock this afternoon at that so-called church of his. I told him you were in big trouble with the law and to keep it under his hat. Of course, I didn't tell him I was sending Lenny in my place."

"Oh, God," said Elaine.

"And to be on the safe side I told him to bring along your little friend from the Eighth Street Grill. You know, the one with the orange Volkswagen. I couldn't be sure what she knew."

"Hadley, you're insane," said Arnold. "You'll wind up killing half the population of New York."

Hadley yawned and drew Sherry close to him as he backed into the bedroom.

"I'll see you two in a couple of hours," he said, kicking the door shut. "Sorry I don't have any magazines for you to read while you wait."

Chapter 17

For the first few minutes after they had been left alone Arnold and Elaine sat in silence, staring at the bedroom door in horror. Finally Elaine turned her head and faced Arnold.

"Arnie, they actually mean to kill us."

Put as simply as that it sounded incredible, fantastic. Arnold had known Hadley for more than twenty years. He could remember standing next to him at Yale-Harvard games, drinking from Hadley's flask and singing "Boola-Boola." It did not seem possible it had come to this.

"What are we going to do?"

The question brought him face to face with the reality of their situation. What, indeed, were they going to do?

"See if you can reach over and touch my hands. See if you can untie the rope on my wrists."

It was a scene familiar to him from a dozen childhood movies. The two good guys, side by side, hands tied behind their backs, reaching over to loosen one another's bonds. He had used it himself to rescue the hero of an early A. A. Carruthers novel from the clutches of his captor. Its only flaw was that it did not work. Strain though they might, twist and stretch his arm though he did, to the point where it seemed about to break from its socket, he and Elaine could do no more than brush fingertips.

"It's hopeless," he said finally. "We'll have to think of something else."

He twisted violently in his chair in an attempt to loosen his bonds. Every motion served only to tighten the grip in which he was held. The cord cut into his wrist, his arms ached, exhaustion and frustration brought him to the edge of tears.

From the bedroom every now and then came the hoarse sound of Sherry Windsor's laughter and the rhythmic creaking of old bedsprings. Once they heard her cry out, "Hadley! What the hell are you doing? Are you nuts? Oh, God! Oh! Oh!" Arnold looked questioningly at Elaine, but she averted her eyes and stared at the floor.

After a while the room grew silent, and, a few minutes later, Sherry emerged from the bedroom brushing her hair. She smiled coyly at Arnold.

"I think old Hadley will sleep pretty good," she said.

"You don't think you can possibly get away with this, do you?" Arnold asked her. "I mean, Hadley seems to have gone off his rocker, but . . ."

"Oh come off it, Arnold. That's what they always say in movies. Why shouldn't we get away with it?"

"Well, to begin with, don't you think the police are going to be a little suspicious of all these murders connected with the Charnoff agency? They'll start looking for a motive, and where do you suppose that will lead?"

"Oh but Arnold, we've given them a motive. That's where Hadley's so smart. Don't you think he's smart?"

"What motive?" asked Arnold, ignoring her question.

"Why, drug dealing, of course. The police already suspect you of being mixed up with the mob, and Hermie and Matt Pendleton were up to their teeth in it. When they find your bodies they'll just figure that you got caught in the middle of a gang war. That's why Hadley had Lenny plant all those drugs in your apartment."

"My apartment?"

"Sure. When he burglarized it last Tuesday night. He took away all your Alice Smythereene papers and planted a big stash of heroin around your apartment. Also he left some documents that Hadley says will link you up to Big Augie Mancuso."

She began to giggle.

"You'll be famous, Arnold."

"And what about Lenny?" Arnold asked. "I suppose his death will also be written off as a gang slaying. Of course, that makes sense. Poor Lenny."

"I don't wanna talk about it."

Sherry stopped smiling. She began to buff her nails, giving them all her concentration.

"In sickness and in health, for better or for worse until death us do part," Arnold intoned. "Did you pledge that to Lenny when you married him?"

Sherry looked up sharply.

"Who the hell told you about that? How did you know I was married to Lenny? Hadley said he'd fix it so there wasn't any record."

"Well, even the great brain slips up now and then. But think about it. If I found out, how long do you think it's going to take the police?"

Sherry was visibly upset by Arnold's revelation. She stopped buffing her nails and gazed in consternation at the bedroom door as if wondering whether to wake Hadley and have him join the discussion. At length, however, she shook off her indecisiveness and spoke to Arnold in a defiant tone.

"Anyway, it doesn't matter what the police find out about Lenny and I. They can't pin anything on me. The fact is I've been out of town the whole time everything's been going on."

"Out of town?"

"Yeah. Down in the Florida Keys. On vacation. A dozen people have seen me. In fact, I'm still registered at my hotel. They think I'm off on a three-day fishing trip. By ten o'clock tonight I'll be on a plane back down there."

"Wait a minute," said Arnold. "Let me understand this. You mean that all the time you've been 'missing' you've been down in Florida?"

"Sure. Where do you think I got this gorgeous tan? It was Hadley's idea. As long as I was reported missing anyway, he decided we could make use of it. So right after we got rid of Herman I got on a plane for Florida and found an out-of-the-way hotel in the Keys. Of course, I registered under an assumed name, the idea being that Alice Smythereene felt the need to get away and be alone for a while. And I haven't seen a newspaper or watched TV for weeks—I wanted to get away from everything—so I didn't even know there was any fuss over my disappearance. Get it?"

"That way Alice Smythereene isn't compromised by any of the dirty business touching the Herman Charnoff agency," said Arnold. "I have to admit it's a clever idea."

"Of course it is," agreed Sherry. "I told you Hadley was smart. Then in a week or so I return to New York very apologetic about having raised such a fuss and scared everybody by my disappearance. It gets a big play in the papers, and later on, when all the bodies are found and the police figure out when they were killed, well, I was in Florida during that period."

She returned her attention to her fingernails.

"I think I'll polish them. I just bought a new shade of hot pink. It ought to really go with this tan, don't you think?"

"You're amazing, Sherry," said Elaine. "But there's one thing I don't understand. What are you doing back here? Why didn't you stay in Florida? Couldn't you find enough men there to screw?"

Sherry smiled at her.

"You know, honey, I'm gonna be sort of sorry to see old Arnold get it. He's really kind of sweet. But I think I'll enjoy watching you get killed."

She began polishing the fingernails of her left hand.

"But in answer to your question, I had to come back for a few days because Lenny was getting out of control. He doesn't like Hadley, you know, and he just wouldn't do what he was told. Of course, he'll do whatever I tell him. As long as he thinks it's gonna bring me back to him."

She blew on her left hand for a few seconds before continuing.

"I mean all that business about blowing up that car. And coming after poor Arnold in the street like that. That was all Lenny's idea. Very crude, don't you think? Not the way Hadley wanted to do it at all. Hadley's much too suave for those kind of tricks, don't you think so?"

Having finished her left hand she began to polish her right.

It was late afternoon before Hadley rejoined them.

"My goodness," he said, looking at his watch. "A quarter to three. I didn't intend to sleep that long."

He stretched and yawned. Sherry sat on the couch looking thoughtful. Her mind had obviously returned to Lenny.

"Hey, I thought you were going to fix it so that nobody could connect me up with Lenny."

"And so I shall, my pet. Don't you worry your pretty little head about it."

Come Back, Alice Smythereene! 169

He reached out to give her a reassuring pat, but she avoided his touch.

"It seems to me like it's already too late," she said.

"Why don't you just leave everything to me," said Hadley with an air of closing the discussion.

Sherry frowned.

"You know, Had," said Arnold. "You've overlooked one important item."

"Oh, and what's that?"

"If you kill me and let Sherry take over as Alice Smythereene, who is going to write the stories from now on? Have you thought of that?"

"Indeed I have," replied Hadley glibly. "I should think the answer's obvious. Can't you guess?"

Arnold paused to think.

"Sherry herself?"

Hadley snorted, which roused his true love's ire.

"What's the matter? Don't you think I could write them?" she demanded. "I could do as well as anybody."

"Of course you could, darling," said Hadley soothingly. "It's just that you'll be so busy with personal appearances you won't have time. Oh come on, Arnold. Surely you can guess who's going to be the writing member of the team."

"Hadley! You?" scoffed Arnold. "Don't make me laugh. You can't write romances. You don't have the knack."

"That's where you're wrong," said Hadley. "Dead wrong. I fact, I've already written several chapters of Alice Smythereene's next opus. They're in my briefcase in the car. Wait a minute, I'll get them."

He hurried outside.

"I think I'm going mad," said Elaine. "Or else this is all a bad dream."

Hadley was back, waving a manuscript.

"Here it is, Arn. Do you want to read it? Actually, I wouldn't mind getting your opinion on a few points."

Elaine stared at him.

"I think I'm going to be sick," she said.

"I'd love to read it, Had, but—well, I'm a little tied up at the moment."

He smiled at his friend, who, after a moment, began to chuckle.

"Arn, I have to admire you. You've got lots of aplomb. I'll tell you what. I can untie your arms but leave your legs and torso tied to the chair. That way you can read. How's that?"

"Well . . ."

"And while you're doing that, Sherry can find something for us to eat."

It was Sherry's turn to snort.

"Huh! Find something yourself. I don't feel like cooking."

"Oh now, precious . . ."

"Don't precious me. I'm tired of being treated like a servant around here. And like a dummy. You understand? I can write and talk as well as anybody else. Let *her* do the cooking."

She jabbed her finger viciously at Elaine.

"Don't be silly," said Hadley.

"Well, it's an idea," said Arnold. "Elaine knows her way around this kitchen, and I'm sure she can come up with something."

Elaine was dumbfounded.

Arnold went on. "If we have a few eggs in the house and some cheese, Elaine can work up a beautiful quiche. One last good meal together, ol' bulldog buddy, and then good-bye, with no hard feelings."

At the word "quiche" Hadley's face momentarily lighted.

"I remember a quiche we had in your house about a

year ago," he told Elaine. "Do you remember it? It had Camembert cheese with walnuts in it. God, it was splendid."

His face fell.

"I don't think we have the proper ingredients to do Elaine justice. And I'm not so naive, my foolish friend, as not to think you are trying to set up some trick. But this isn't one of your silly A. A. Carruthers yarns, you know."

"Look, Had," said Arnold, lowering his voice and looking earnestly at his friend. "I wouldn't ask anything for myself, but I don't think Elaine can take much more. Those ropes are cutting off her circulation. It's inhuman, Had. Look how sick she is. Can't you untie her for a bit?"

"I wish I could, Arn. Really I do, but . . ."

"Where's she going to go? You two have the guns. I'll tell you what. You untie Elaine, let her walk around a bit and get her circulation back. She can make us some dinner while Sherry stands guard over her. In the meantime I'll go over your manuscript."

"I don't know, Arn. Maybe if Elaine would give us her word . . ."

He looked questioningly at Sherry.

"Her word? Are you nuts? You think this is Yale College? This is no friggin' game. This is for real."

Arnold saw Hadley stiffen at her words.

"That may be, but there's no point in being inhumane."

"I can't see you treating a woman that way, Had," Arnold told him.

"You're right, Arn."

Hadley began untying Elaine.

"Noblesse oblige, after all," he said.

It took several minutes of stretching and bending before Elaine was able to walk.

"I've got to go to the bathroom," she said.

It was a contingency Hadley had not planned for.

"Oh yes, of course," he said. Then, to Sherry he added, "You'd better stay with her and make sure she doesn't try to get out the window."

"For Chrissake," she replied. "First I'm supposed to be a friggin' cook. Now I'm a nursemaid."

She followed Elaine to the bathroom.

> Lord Havisham dipped a forefinger into his glass of champagne, then moved it slowly toward the rosy nipple of the supine maiden.

"Hadley, this won't do," said Arnold authoritatively. "Supine maiden? Nobody's said supine maiden for a hundred years. And Lord Havisham sounds like a name out of P. G. Wodehouse. This is romance, Had. Also, rosy nipple is a tad cliché, don't you think?"

Hadley gave him a hurt look.

"Well, it's my first effort, and I haven't had time to revise it yet."

Arnold shook his head.

"Sorry, Had. You're going to have to do better than this. There's an art to writing these things. Not everyone can do it. Don't get me wrong. The Rick Rheingold stuff was wonderful in its way, but this is something different."

"I can learn," said Hadley defensively.

Arnold read in silence for the next ten minutes. From the kitchen came the smell of bacon frying.

"Hadley," said Arnold, laying down the manuscript, "there's something I've been meaning to ask you. Was Farner really working for the mob, or was that something you made up?"

"I just told you that to raise your suspicions," answered Hadley. "Keep you from calling him, you know? I had Lenny use his name when he called Elaine with the story of you being run over. Just to throw you off. As far as I know Farner is an honest cop. Eccentric, maybe. But honest."

Arnold read on.

"Hadley," he said after a few minutes. "Do you really think the reader is going to be interested in four pages of seafood recipes from Regency England?"

"I put a lot of research into that," Hadley answered. "And I'm writing for a discerning readership."

"You're writing for Alice Smythereene's readership. And, with all due modesty, there's no one who knows that audience like I do. I could improve your manuscript a lot if you'd let me make some changes. Do you have a pen?"

"Sure, Arn. I'd appreciate it."

"First, however, I have to go to the bathroom."

Hadley eyed him suspiciously.

"It happens to all of us, Had. I can't help it. And the cardinal rule of romance writing is not to attempt it on a full bladder."

"Just don't try anything," said Hadley. "Don't forget that I have this gun, Arn. And I won't hesitate to use it, believe me."

"I believe you, Had."

Hadley untied him, then followed him, gun at the ready, to the bathroom. He stood in the doorway, leaning against the jamb, watching Arnold.

"Not the most delicate arrangement, is it?" Arnold asked.

"Sorry, Arn, but I've got to make sure you don't go out the window."

He relieved himself under Hadley's watchful eye. As he washed his hands afterwards he stood so close to him that he could have reached out and touched the gun had he had the nerve. Instead he stared at the basin, concentrating on what he knew to be in the cabinet beneath.

Oh God, he thought, let him be distracted, even for an instant.

Arnold's prayer was answered by a scream from the kitchen.

"You bitch!" It was Sherry's voice. "I ought to kill you right now for that!"

"What's going on?" called Hadley.

As he said it he turned his head slightly in the direction of the kitchen. It was all Arnold needed. He shoved Hadley out of the doorway, then slammed and locked the door.

"She tried to splatter hot bacon grease in me," he heard Sherry screaming. "I told you . . ."

"Never mind that now," shouted Hadley. "Get outside and cover the bathroom window. Shoot him if he tries to climb out. Hurry up! Leave Elaine in here with me. I'll cover her. Hurry!"

There was a sound of running, then he heard the front door banging open. Arnold dropped to his knees in front of the sink.

"Elaine, don't move or I'll kill you," said Hadley on the other side of the bathroom door. "Now, Arnold, don't be so damned childish. What good is locking yourself in the bathroom going to do? I still have Elaine here. You're not just going to desert her, are you? Shame on you. Be a good boy and open up."

Arnold felt along the back of the sink cabinet until he found what he was seeking. The can of lye was there where he remembered it.

"I'm back here, Hadley," came Sherry's voice through the open bathroom window. "He's not out here."

Thank God, thought Arnold, it's too high for her to look through. He removed the top of the can, and, reaching up, held it under the faucet. With his other hand he turned the tap and let a trickle of water run into the half-filled can.

"Okay, Arnold, I'm through fooling around. I'm

counting three. If you're not out by then, first Elaine gets it, then I shoot open the door. One."

With his left hand Arnold gently swirled the can of lye. With his right he grabbed the only other weapon available, the plunger that stood alongside the sink.

"Two."

"Okay, Hadley. You win. I'm coming out."

He gripped the plunger near its base and positioned the handle under the door hook. Then he lifted the hook out of the eye. The door swung inward for an inch or so, and he opened it the rest of the way with his foot. "Arnold, I'm surprised—"

He threw the lye at Hadley's face, at the same time smashing the plunger handle against the knuckles of Hadley's gun hand.

"Elaine!" he shouted. "Lock the front door!"

As he shouted he threw his shoulder into Hadley.

"Oh my God!" screamed Hadley. "I can't see! Sherry, help me!"

The gun fell from Hadley's hand as he doubled over in pain, holding his face with both hands. Arnold mustered all his strength and drove his fist into Hadley's stomach. Then he dropped on all fours and scrambled after the gun.

"Lemme in there, you son of a bitch, or I'll blow your fuckin' head off!" screamed Sherry Windsor from outside the front door. To punctuate her words a blast of gunfire shattered the windowpane nearest the door.

"Elaine, are you all right?" Arnold shouted.

Before she could answer, there was a second gunshot and a noise of smashing glass. He felt a blow like the stroke of a sledgehammer against his shoulder. It spun him around and threw him backward to the wall. The gun fell out of his hands.

"Oh my God! Arnie!" screamed Elaine.

From the opposite side of the room came the sound of Hadley, whimpering.

"Oh, please. Somebody help me. I can't see! My eyes are burning. I need cold water for my eyes. Please."

Outside it was quiet. Sherry had stopped firing. As Arnold listened he caught the sound of a car engine drawing closer, then two blasts of an automobile horn.

Oh my God, he thought. It's Manuszak, come back to finish us off.

The pain in his shoulder was intense, and he felt as though he were about to faint. Through bleary eyes he saw Hadley crawling along the floor, one hand to his eyes, the other groping in front of him. He could hear Elaine crying.

From outside came more sounds of gunshots, further away than before. He heard, as in a dream, the shout "Halt!" echoing in the distance. A pool of blood had gathered at the spot where his right shoulder touched the ground, and the sight of it made him sick to his stomach. Everything went black before him, and the last thing he was conscious of before passing out was a voice from outside shouting into the cabin.

"Throw down your guns in there and come out with your hands up! This is the police! We have the place surrounded. Simon, are you all right? This is Farner."

Chapter 18

"You were very brave, Arnie."

Elaine was sitting on the edge of his bed. Behind her, like a big black giant, loomed Farner.

"Where am I?" he asked.

"Wilmington, Vermont, Professor," answered Farner. "In the hospital. You had a thirty-eight slug taken out of your shoulder last night."

"You'll be fine," said Elaine. "The doctor says you'll be up and around in a couple of days."

"It was lucky my getting there when I did," said Farner. "Not that you needed much help. You did pretty well on your own, Professor Simon. Still and all, we were lucky."

Arnold's throat was dry.

"Could I have something to drink?" he asked.

Elaine held a cup of water out to him, and he drank through a bent straw. When he had finished he looked up at Farner.

"How did you find us?"

"Well, sir, we owe it to Luther. He got a little nervous in the early hours of yesterday morning, nervous about Mrs. Simon, I mean. The same as you did. So he called Miss Michelson, and she told him the same thing she had

177

told you. How I had called Mrs. Simon with some cock-and-bull story about you being in an accident. Only, Luther knew you hadn't been in any accident, and he also knew I wouldn't have lied about it."

Farner smiled at Arnold.

"Uh, Sergeant, I'm sorry about doubting you. It's not that I ever thought you were dishonest, it's just . . ."

"Don't give it another thought, Professor. Lord knows we all get our heads full of stories about crooked cops from books and television. And from real life, too, I suppose.

"Well anyway, Luther called and told me about it, and we put our heads together to try and figure out what was happening. Then when Luther got a phone call from Ottinger, things sort of clicked."

"But how did you know we were in Vermont?"

"That took a bit of doing. To begin with, Luther suspected from something Ottinger said that he was calling from out of town. Then it occurred to me that he might have used a credit card to make the call, and we let the phone company take it from there. I must say they worked fast. Of course, when we discovered that the call was placed from Wilmington, Vermont, and Luther told me of your summer place near here, it was pretty obvious where you must be."

Arnold took another sip of water. He opened his mouth to ask another question but was stopped by Elaine.

"Arnie, I think you ought to rest. You can talk to Sergeant Farner later."

"I just wanted to ask about Luther and Francine. Are they all right?"

"They're fine, sir. Of course, we realized immediately that Ottinger was up to something when he made that appointment with Luther, so we had the Temple of Vishnu loaded with police at the appointed hour. We didn't know we'd bag Manuszak, but we thought we'd get something to make it worth our while. I didn't wait, though. I phoned ahead to the Vermont state police and then hightailed it up here as fast as I could."

"Sergeant, I'm indebted to you. I guess there's no way I can repay you."

"Well, I wouldn't say that, Professor. You see, I have a manuscript I've been working on—a novel, that is—and when you're feeling better, perhaps . . ."

He was stopped short by a glare from Elaine.

"Well, that can wait, sir. No hurry about it. I'll wait for you outside, Mrs. Simon."

When he had left the room Elaine bent down and kissed Arnold lightly on the lips.

"Oh Arnie, I was so frightened. I thought we were going to die. You were actually heroic."

"Elaine, I told you if we got out of it I'd make it up to you. And I'm going to. Anything you want me to do, I'll do."

"Right now, I just want you to get well."

"No, Elaine. I mean it. Anything you want from now on. You want to move back to Brooklyn? We'll move back to Brooklyn. You want me to stop writing trash? I'll stop writing trash."

"We'll talk about it later. Right now you need to get some rest."

"The worst part of the whole business was the thought of anything bad happening to you. I couldn't have stood it. I love you so much, Elaine."

"Oh Arnie, you big jerk. I love you too."

She was crying. He took it as a sign that everything would be all right.

Arnold looked out the window at the snow falling on Fifth Avenue. The party was going well, but he was tired and hoped it would be over soon. It occurred to him that this was the first time in years that Herman Charnoff had not been at their annual Christmas party. Or Hadley Ottinger, for that matter.

He was startled to hear the lawyer's name spoken aloud.

"Hadley Ottinger. What's happened to him, Arnold?" It was Beverly Michelson asking the question. "Was he permanently blinded?"

"No," he answered. "The police got there in time to rinse his eyes out pretty well. He does have impaired vision, though. Always will. I feel a little bad about that."

"Oh come on, now. He was trying to kill you."

"Well, I know, but . . ."

"Not to mention the fact that he's suing us for half a million dollars," said Elaine as she joined them. "For damage to his eyes inflicted by Arnold's malicious attack. Can you imagine?"

"Well, still I feel a little sorry for him," insisted Arnold. "Anyway, he's got his own trial coming up to worry about."

Out of the corner of his eye Arnold saw the large figure of Henry Farner at the other end of the room. He wanted to have a word with the detective.

"Excuse me for a minute, will you, Bev?"

He moved toward Farner, but his progress was stopped by a buxom lady of sixty-odd years. Arnold recognized her as belonging somehow to the neighborhood, perhaps a fellow occupant of their building.

"Oh, Professor, I hear you'll be leaving us soon."

"Yes. We're moving back to Brooklyn Heights in the spring. We own a brownstone there."

He tried to move past, but she put a hand on his arm.

"Have you sold this apartment yet? If not, I know someone who might be interested in buying it."

"As a matter of fact, we're not going to sell it for a

while. We're renting it out to friends. Here they are, in fact."

He motioned to Luther and Francine, who were standing at the punchbowl a few feet away.

"Luther! Francine! Could you step over here for a minute? I'd like you to meet one of your new neighbors, Mrs., uh . . ."

"Wigfall. Naomi Wigfall."

Mrs. Wigfall eyed Luther and Francine with suspicion.

"Mrs. Wigfall, may I present Luther Washington and Francine?"

Once again he had forgotten Francine's last name. Oh well, he thought, it doesn't matter. He would just think of her as Francine Washington.

"Luther and Francine are authors," he told Mrs. Wigfall. "They write romance novels. Under what name, Luther?"

"Blanche LeNoir, my dear lady," said Luther in his oiliest tone. "We've just finished our first. It's being published in the spring, and I do hope you will accept an autographed copy with our compliments."

"Ooh, I just love romance," gushed Mrs. Wigfall.

Arnold skirted her and headed toward Farner.

"Well, there. And how is Washington Square's own Barbara Cartland?"

It was Vance Lovejoy, his department chairman, blocking his way.

"Ah come on, Vance. Lay off. I'm through with that. I promised Elaine."

Arnold was famous. The case had made headlines in the papers and had even been written up in *Time*. He had endured months of tasteless ribbing from friends and colleagues.

"Decided to retire on your millions, eh?"

"I doubt that there will be any millions. In fact I'm inclined to think there won't be any money at all by the time all the litigation is finished. The network dropped the mini-series, you know. Too controversial. And Sherry Windsor is still claiming to be the real Alice Smythereene. That one will be years in court, and by the time it's over I'm sure the lawyers will have any money that's left."

"Oh well, maybe your book on minor Victorian poets will hit it big."

Lovejoy laughed explosively. Then, when his laughter had subsided, he moved closer to Arnold and asked in a low tone, "Tell me, Arnie, are those things hard to write? I've had an idea for a story for a long time now. Been carrying it around in my head, and I . . ."

"Why don't you ask Luther Washington? He just finished one. You remember Luther, don't you? He's over there."

He pointed to where Luther and Francine stood talking to the enraptured Mrs. Wigfall.

"Excuse me, Vance. I've got to see someone."

He reached Farner just as the detective was putting on his coat.

"Well, Sergeant, leaving so early? I haven't had a chance to talk to you."

"Heavy day tomorrow, Professor. Thanks for inviting me. By the way, did you get a chance to look at my manuscript?"

"That's what I wanted to talk to you about. But look, don't you think we know each other well enough by now to drop the Professor and Sergeant routine? Why don't you just call me Arnold?"

"It'll be a privilege, Arnold." Farner extended his hand. "Call me Henry."

They shook hands.

"About your story, Henry. It's really very interesting. Needs some work, a professional touch. I'd like to talk to you at length about it. Are you free for lunch some day next week?"

Henry and Arnold, he thought. It was more appropriate that way. Collaborators should be on an informal basis.

"How about Wednesday, Arnold?"

"Wednesday's fine. I'll call you." They shook hands again. "Oh, and Henry—I think it might be better if Elaine didn't know anything about this for a while. Until I find the right moment to tell her."

Farner smiled.

"I understand," he said.

Arnold moved on, circling the room, stopping now and then to chat with one of his guests. He returned to the group at the window in time to hear Elaine saying, "No. Arnold's finished with that. No more romance, no more thrillers. Just scholarship and poetry, thank God."

She leaned against me and put her arms around my neck.
"Don't let them put me away, Mike," she whispered in my ear. "You and me, we can make beautiful music together."
I looked at the smoking thirty-eight in my hand and then down at her dead boyfriend at my feet. In the distance I could hear sirens.
"Sorry, baby," I told her.

A bit crude, to be sure. It lacked polish and the style was imitative. But Farner's story was exciting, the narrative was vigorous and interesting. And the idea of a series featuring a black private eye teamed up with a white policewoman was certainly timely.

He made notes in the margin as he read. Together, he thought, with Farner's sense of narrative and his sense of style, they could really have something big. A blockbuster. With movie and television sales. He felt sure that Farner would agree to a partnership.

He listened to Elaine singing in the shower. *La Traviata.* Always a sign that she was happy. The party had gone well. Their lives were going well. They were together again and that was what counted. No point in spoiling things by talking about his plans for Farner and himself. Plenty of time for that after they had a finished manuscript in their hands. Better yet, a sale.

Elaine had turned off the shower. Arnold could hear her voice more clearly now. He put the manuscript in the drawer of his desk, pushing it as far back as he could. Then he went into the bedroom to wait for Elaine.

It occurred to him that they would need a pseudonym, he and Farner. He relaxed and let his mind wander over various possibilities, but he was too tired to come up with anything. Ah well, no matter. He'd think of something tomorrow.